INFRA DIG

*I*NFRA

*D*IG

RALPH MCINERNY

ATHENEUM
NEW YORK 1992
MAXWELL MACMILLAN CANADA
TORONTO
MAXWELL MACMILLAN INTERNATIONAL
NEW YORK OXFORD SINGAPORE SYDNEY

Copyright © 1992 by Ralph McInerny

Atheneum   Maxwell Macmillan Canada, Inc.
Macmillan Publishing Company   1200 Eglinton Avenue East
866 Third Avenue   Suite 200
New York, NY 10022   Don Mills, Ontario M3C 3N1

Macmillan Publishing Company is part of the Maxwell Communication Group of Companies.

Library of Congress Cataloging-in-Publication Data
McInerny, Ralph M.
    Infra Dig / Ralph McInerny.
        p.   cm.
    ISBN 0-689-12132-6
    I. Title.
    PS3563.A31166I5   1991
    813'.54—dc20   91-37334   CIP

10 9 8 7 6 5 4 3 2 1

Printed in the United States of America

For Theresa and Mike Coulombe

PART ONE

1

LEAVES, GOLD, blood red, tan and yellow, spun in the crisp
October air, some still clinging to the trees, others already
spiraling down. Susan stopped when she came out of the
town library and almost cried out in delight at the sight of
this autumn world. This was her favorite season. It had been
Harry's too. She inhaled deeply and caught the faintest hint
of burning leaves, someone ignoring the town ordinance,
thank God. What was fall without the smell of burning
leaves?

She stepped aside as the door opened and little Amy
Rordam came out smiling her chipmunk smile. She put her
hand on Susan's arm.

"And how is Frederick?"

"He asked about you." It seemed an unimportant lie when
Susan considered the pleasure it gave Amy.

"I must come see him."

"He'd like that."

"Of course I'd want to come when you're there, Susan."

Susan did not smile. Amy Rordam's sense of propriety was what one expected. Belting, Wisconsin, might have been all but swallowed up by Milwaukee now, but it retained the small-town mores that had brought Susan and Harry back here in the first year of their marriage. Her mother was still alive then and both his parents. Now only Fred was left. Susan and Fred. Orphaned and widowed and responsible for her invalid father-in-law, Susan felt more at home in Belting, not less. To live where one's dead were buried did not seem a morbid thought.

"I'll call you, Amy."

The older woman took Susan's hand. "Honestly, I feel so guilty not being more help to you. I know how difficult Fred must be."

"I can be pretty difficult myself."

Amy made a little puffing noise, dismissing this. They had started down the walk when Amy put her hand on Susan's arm, stopping her. Jogging toward them, his running shorts flapping at his flanks, tee shirt pasted with perspiration to his bony chest, came Will Tonsor, grinning like a death's head. When he reached them, he began to run in place, his bright eyes darting between the younger and older woman.

"Good afternoon, ladies!" He expelled the words on his panting breath.

Susan nodded, wishing he would stop and rest. His complexion was either very healthy or evidence of high blood pressure. Apple-red cheeks, white hair lying damp and spiky on his narrow pink forehead, matching white mustache. But it was Amy's attention he wanted. And did not get. She continued down the walk, and Susan went with her.

"The old fool will kill himself, trying to frisk about like a boy." Amy spoke through clenched teeth. She seemed genuinely angry.

"I think he's showing off for you, Amy."

"Don't joke about it," Amy said sternly. She glanced at Susan, then looked quickly away. "Please."

Will Tonsor was where they had left him, knees pumping, bright eyes trained on Amy. Susan waved and this set him on his way. Beside her, Amy made an impatient noise.

"Thank God Fred acts his age, Susan."

It was all Susan could do not to protest. Will Tonsor might look foolish, jogging himself into the pink, but to Susan that seemed preferable to her father-in-law's valetudinarian grumbling. She must invite Amy over, if only to dispel her illusions about Frederick Nebens.

When Amy refused a ride Susan wended her way through the parking lot to her car, a huge ten-year-old station wagon with rusting fenders and a tendency to burn oil. She should get a newer, more economical car. But when she sold the station wagon there would be one less link with her life with Harry.

She pulled open the driver's door and tossed her books onto the seat. Before getting in herself she looked over the roof of the car at Amy Rordam still standing where they had parted. The older woman lifted a tentative hand and waved. Had Amy just stood there, watching Susan go to her car, wearing the expression she wore as she waved? Pity? Sympathy? What? Whatever it was, Susan didn't like to think of herself as an object of concern. The Widow Nebens, is that how Amy thought of her? Suddenly Susan had a vision of how the whole town saw her, the woman who had seemed so lucky to marry Harry Nebens. She had been over thirty at the time, no prize, whereas Harry . . . After such good luck had come the bad. Harry dead in his forties. But whatever pity Amy and others might feel for her would be caused by the fact that Susan had ended up with Harry's father, Fred, on her hands.

She started the motor and waited for the vibration of the muffler to stop before putting the car in gear and starting out of the parking lot. Amy Rordam was no longer in sight.

The house was filled with the smell of pipe tobacco. Susan left the front door open and went through to the kitchen. Fred was sitting on the patio, in his wheelchair, holding a match to his pipe. She would bet he had rolled outside when he heard the car. The pipe was already lit. She slid open the screen door and went onto the patio. He lurched and turned with a surprise she knew was feigned.

"Good God, you scared me."

"I saw Amy Rordam at the library."

"I didn't know she could read."

"She wants to come see you."

He leaned forward to look past her, as if fearful Amy had come home with her. Satisfied Susan was alone, he said, "Tell her I'm not home." He paused. "Tell her I've gone away."

"Gone away! Where?"

He lifted soulful eyes, stared at her for a moment and then looked down.

"Bowling?" she suggested.

"Ha! Sure, tell her I've gone bowling."

"Maybe she'd want to go along."

"You know I don't bowl!" he shouted, genuinely angry. "I never bowled in my life." He twisted away and looked out over the back lawn.

Susan went inside and put on coffee. She shouldn't tease Fred. It was all right for him to say silly things to her, but if she replied in kind he became angry. He was angry most of the time now, and she was the object of his rage at the world. Fred was waiting to die, there was no other way to describe his life. It was a thought made sadder by the fear that, in a way, it described her own life as well.

Waiting in the kitchen for the coffee to boil, she stared through the window, not really seeing anything. Her house had become the place she least liked to be, and there was no point in pretending to herself that Fred wasn't the reason. This admission was made deep inside her, well below the level where thoughts are transmitted to the face and betray themselves in expressions. Could anyone really imagine how difficult it was to live with Fred? How could they, when he put on such an act whenever others were around? Jovial old Fred, full of cracker-barrel wisdom, self-deprecation and constant praise of Susan. He was a cunning old man, malevolent, a man who hated his dependence on her more than she resented having become his keeper.

On the porch a hacking cough was heard, the forced rasping sound Fred had developed over the past several weeks. He would wheel into the room, get her attention and hold up his hand, eyes shut, breathing rapidly through his nose, and then it would begin, the apparently helpless choking cough. It was an alarming sound, but even more it was intensely aggravating because Susan was certain he was coughing on purpose. The terrible sound went on and on, an indictment and accusation, but of whom? Of her, of course. How could she be forgiven all the help she had given him? But the target was much wider than that. Fred hated the universe for what had happened to him. He hated God.

"Don't say that!" Susan cried out when he first said that.

"Do you think it really matters whether we say we hate or love Him?"

"You know it does."

"Maybe it matters to us, but what does He care? If He had an eye on the world do you think things would be as bad as they are, poverty, disease, war . . ."

"Old age?"

That struck home. His wild, rheumy eyes stared at her, he breathed through his slack, open mouth, an old man, sunk into himself, skeletal spotted hands gripping the rubberized wheels of his chair. He spun 180 degrees and rolled out of the kitchen and onto the porch.

They teased one another, that's what it came down to, although teasing made it sound like an innocent game.

"You should marry again," he said.

"Is that a proposal?"

"You already have me."

"Maybe *you* should marry again, Fred."

"Who would have me?"

"Good question."

"What the hell does that mean?"

"Did you have someone in mind?"

"Listen, there are plenty of women in this town who would jump at the chance."

The irony was that he was probably right. Well, maybe not plenty, but there were one or two, Amy Rordam for instance.

"I could ask them to come calling," Susan said sweetly. Oh, she hated herself when she got into these silly exchanges with the old man. "How about Amy Rordam?"

"That old bitch."

It infuriated Susan that he should talk that way about someone as sweet and good as Amy. But the absurd quarrel started her dreaming of what her own life could be like if she were free of the burden of her father-in-law. It would be a dirty trick to play on someone like Amy, but one read of such unions frequently enough, a couple in their seventies, marrying out of loneliness and the need for companionship. Maybe Amy would welcome even a cranky Fred in preference to being all alone.

But whatever pity Susan summoned for Amy seemed to be directed at herself as well. Both of them needed the volunteer work they did in order to keep sane. What was considered Susan's generosity was in large part her desire to get out of the house and away from Fred. He knew that even if no one else did, and he resented it. However much he hated her he wanted her there to tease, to annoy, to aggravate.

"Can I get you something?" she cried out as the coughing on the porch continued.

He caught himself in the middle of a choking cough. "What?"

Susan squeezed her eyes shut and said nothing.

"You say something?"

"Coffee's ready. Want a cup?"

"Put some hemlock in it."

When people visited, it was his idea of a joke to pretend that she was trying to get rid of him, putting arsenic in his soup, ground glass in his hamburger, threatening to wheel him down to the river and dump him off the bridge. People laughed, but Susan could see the mean glint in his eye as he watched them. What did he want? Expressions of outrage and disbelief at the thought that Fred Nebens could actually cease to be? Will Tonsor was Susan's ally in kidding Fred.

"Just take him out with the trash, Susan," he suggested. "Prop him up with the rest of it and they'll cart him away."

"We'll go together," Fred cried playfully.

"After you, my dear Gaston." And Will stood, all six and a half feet of him, and bowed.

It was difficult to believe the two men were the same age. Oh, if only Fred were still able to get about the way Will did, life would be so different. Will still golfed, he ran a mile or two every day, he swam at the Y. Fred made an Olympic event out of his weekly bath.

2

WILL TONSOR had made his money in both real estate and insurance. His wife left him before their fourth anniversary, and the fact was he never missed her. She stayed with a sister in Skokie before moving to Fresno, where she remarried and dropped completely out of his life. The freedom this gave him for business enabled him to achieve economic comfort and then wealth. In his fifties, he sold his combined realty company and insurance agency and devoted himself to managing his money. A fateful decision. Several unwise investments had depleted his capital dramatically, but Carter era interest rates—disastrous for borrowers, lovely for savers— had enabled him to recoup. The unease brought on by this brush with economic disaster might have made him susceptible to religion, but it was the carnal itch that all but overcame him.

He tried to remember what it had been like to be married.

The photograph albums his wife had left behind should have triggered off memories, but they did not. His wife seemed a total stranger, not someone with whom he had gone to bed. Had they actually done it? They must have, of course, but he could not remember. Before the great mystery of married life, Will Tonsor felt no more knowledgeable than a boy. He decided to dedicate his remaining years to repairing the damage.

He had known success in business and, up to a point, in financial management, but he proved to have no gift at all for igniting the spark of desire in the tender sex. For nearly two decades he had pursued amorous adventure with only equivocal success. Annually he went on Caribbean cruises which promised adventure and romance but provided only seasickness. He went regularly to Las Vegas, but the reckless tossing about of money depressed him, neutralizing the aphrodisiac of the fleshy floor shows. He spent time at California health ranches whose glossy brochures suggested that forbidden heights of passion were to be found there, but the churning water in the communal baths did not sufficiently conceal the blubbery belles who shared the pool with him. Meanwhile, he took care of himself, keeping his aging body in trim against the day when the vague object of his desire would assume a particular shape. And so she did when in his seventies he realized that the skittish and diminutive Amy Rordam was what his heart desired.

To some degree there was a lack of gallantry in his turning ultimately to Amy. He had sought his love in exotic places; he had pursued his desire among the glitter and glitziness of gambling casinos and sensitivity farms. He could be forgiven for thinking that so relatively modest an objective as Amy Rordam could be quickly conquered. He was wrong. Dead wrong. But bitter as this realization was, it was made more bitter by the fact that Amy seemed to have tender feelings toward Fred Nebens! The man had cut Will's hair for years, they had known one another since school days. It had never occurred to Will that a mere barber could prove to be a rival. He redoubled his efforts to reveal to Amy Rordam the attractiveness of his person, counseled in this effort by Matt Hilliard, manager of the Belting Country Club.

"Bashful," Matt said, rolling out his lower lip and nodding when Will told him of his latest ambiguous encounter with Amy. "You were dressed like that?"

Will sat puffing and perspiring in a captain's chair in the members' bar where he had collapsed after returning from his run. "Yes."

"A woman that age . . ."

"That age!"

"How old is she?"

"Younger than I am."

There was a dangerous moment when Will Tonsor feared Hilliard would say something wounding to their relationship, but the manager looked away. "She never married?"

"No."

"How would you like to be her age and a virgin and then be confronted by the male body in all its splendor?"

Funny fellow, Hilliard, but he had a reputation for giving horizontal interviews to female applicants for jobs at the club. He spoke in a world-weary way of his conquests, and Will Tonsor was sure he was in good hands consulting Hilliard. It did make sense that running into him nearly naked would upset Amy. His own fear was that she would be put off by his long, thin legs, high hips and bony chest. Hilliard's surprising suggestion that he was a concupiscible object to

Amy was a consolation, and he found his discouragement lifting.

"Give the lady a call," Hilliard advised. "Ask her to dinner, here at the club. Put on the dog a little."

Will Tonsor made reservations in the dining room immediately after showering and before he telephoned Amy. It seemed an expression of confidence.

"I never eat out," Amy said.

"I've made reservations at the club."

"The club? What club?"

"The country club."

There was a chilly silence. "My brother was fired as greenskeeper at that club. It ruined his life. He turned to drink, just as . . ."

"Your brother worked here?"

"Years ago."

"Amy, I had nothing to do with that. We'll dine elsewhere."

"No, thank you. Good night, Will Tonsor. Do not imagine that I am in need of companionship. I am sure you mean well, but please do not put yourself out for me."

She hung up. He recalled the conversation for Hilliard and the manager beamed.

"She's on the hook. It's only a matter of time."

Will deferred to the greater knowledge of Matt Hilliard in such matters. He himself would have taken Amy's answer as a definite No.

3

GIVING FRED his bath was the nadir of Susan's week, kneeling beside the tub, soaping the sour body of her tormentor. He would not cover himself with the washcloth, and it became a matter of pride not to keep asking him to. He meant to demean her, she knew that, but she wouldn't give him the satisfaction. It could be worse. If he could get around like Will Tonsor, Fred might be down in the park exposing himself to women and children.

The thought brought a smile to her lips, and it was all she could do not to laugh aloud.

"What's so funny?"

"Nothing." And then the laughter did burst forth. He stared at her in fury. Then he took the washcloth and draped it over his lap. The victory was doubly sweet. Imagine an old man, still full of masculine vanity, in dread of having his impotency referred to.

She got off her knees and stood, trying not to grimace. She had a touch of arthritis but was determined not to let Fred know of it. The skirt she wore had been fashioned from a pair of jeans that had become too tight in the seat. She had slit the legs and sewed them together and, if she remembered her posture, they weren't all bad.

"Where you going?"

"Just sit and soak for a while."

She closed the bathroom door on his profanity. He could sit there until he puckered all over, the nasty old man. She went downstairs and stood at the back door and looked out over her lovely yard. The gardens had been dug and laid out by Harry, he had such a green thumb, and she kept everything just as he had left it. Fred would sit on the back porch in his wheelchair mocking the attention she gave to the flowers and lawn.

"It's something to do."

"What if I needed you when you have that goddam lawn mower going? I can't hear myself think with that thing roaring."

As if he had ever heard himself think. After that she derived a guilty pleasure from the roar of the lawn mower as she directed it over the grass, smiling toward the house from time to time, for Fred's benefit.

Now she spent ten minutes out back, cut a few roses for the vase on the hall table. In the kitchen, running water at the sink, she heard a loud noise. She turned the faucet off and listened. She heard the sound of whimpering.

She ran upstairs to the bathroom and pulled open the door. He lay on the floor beside the tub, his knees pulled up, hugging himself, shivering. She threw a towel over him, then knelt and began to dry the old body.

"What happened?"

"I got out of the tub."

How on earth had he done it alone? Susan was filled with unadulterated guilt now. What was she thinking of, playing games with an old man who couldn't take care of himself? How long had she left him in his bath? Fifteen minutes, possibly more. That was unforgivable. He began to whimper again as she toweled him, and her heart went out to him.

She wrapped him in the bath towel, got her hands under his arms and began to pull him out of the bathroom. How light he was.

"Take it easy," he whined.

"I'll put you to bed."

"Bed? For chrissake, it's afternoon."

She ignored him. He was still shivering. In the hallway she let him down gently, then, with an effort made easy by guilt, actually picked him up and carried him like a baby to his room, ignoring the fierce look of hatred that twisted his face.

"You shouldn't leave me alone."

"You said you didn't want me there when you took your bath."

"I didn't mean you should disappear."

"You're not hurt."

"How do you know?"

"Well, your mouth works all right."

She lay him on the bed and then tried to roll him under the covers the way she had seen nurses do, but she got him all tangled up in the spread and had to put him on the floor and start over again.

"How in hell did I ever end up with you?" he said when she finally had him tucked in.

"I'll make some soup."

"Don't burn it."

People said how sad it was Harry had died so young, but maybe he'd been lucky. She wouldn't have wanted to see him as old as his father, a cranky self-pitying baby.

"What kind of soup is it?" he asked when she brought in the tray.

"Campbells."

He glared at her. "What kind of Campbells?"

He hated tomato, loved consommé. This was chowder, thick, and she'd put a quarter of a box of soda crackers on the tray as well. He liked to set crackers afloat in soup, watch them swell, then eat them with a spoon. He wouldn't be able to do that with the chowder. She went down the hall and waited for him to begin complaining, but there was only the regular slurp of his eating.

She ate the rest of the chowder herself, standing in the kitchen. What a scare he'd given her when she opened the door and saw him crumpled on the bathroom floor. Imagine trying to get out of the tub by himself. He wouldn't get into or out of his wheelchair without assistance, although Doctor Carey had told him he would atrophy if he didn't exercise his limbs. Thanks to the railing, he managed to get up and down the stairs by himself, even though he made a big production out of it if he thought she was watching.

"You think maybe I'll walk again, Doctor?"

"Don't you want to?"

"Anyplace I'm likely to go I've already been."

Doctor Carey had neither the interest nor the patience to nag him about it, and Susan preferred Fred in his chair because then she knew where he was. She even strapped him into it. He liked to wheel silently up behind her to make her jump when he spoke.

It seemed morbid, but Susan sometimes had a vision of an endless future with Fred as he grew more and more helpless and demanding. His wife and son had died young, but, as he often recalled, his father had lived well into his nineties. Photographs of the old man were ominously like Fred: clothes draped over a skeletal figure who seemed propped up for the camera. And the eyes, bright and malevolent. Fred had been wakened as a boy when his father pulled him out of bed.

"By the ears."

"I don't believe you."

He wheeled to her and tipped his head. "You can see where they healed."

She couldn't. She didn't really want to look. Fred seemed to take pleasure in the thought that he was alive while his father was long since dead. Whenever she suggested that he come to the cemetery with her, to visit Harry's grave, he gripped the arms of his chair and shook his head.

"You think he's out there?"

"Fred, people decorate graves on Memorial Day. It's a lovely custom."

She did not try to persuade him. She wanted the time alone by Harry's grave. She didn't think he was there. She wasn't sure where she thought he was, except in her heart. Throughout the cemetery people wandered, carrying flowers, watering cans, standing in silent groups. And it was all right to cry, remembering how wonderful life with Harry had been. Fred had been only a minor nuisance then.

"I want to be cremated," he announced when she came home.

"I thought I'd wait until you're dead."

For the next several days after the tub incident she didn't let him out of her sight, even keeping the bathroom door open when she had him settled on the toilet. The thought kept coming to her that some day she would find him lying dead, in bed, slumped in his chair, somewhere—it was only a matter of time. Thank God, that fall in the bathroom had not been it. She would not have wanted to explain how he had gotten onto the bathroom floor. It would have looked as if he were trying to crawl out of there, to find her, and why wasn't she there when he needed her? Only by turning it into a joke could she let it come out.

4

TWO MORNINGS after the accident, Susan nicked Fred's nose while barbering his nostrils. How hairy an old man he was— hair sprouted from his ears, his brows grew long, antic spears, his nose was particularly luxuriant. The cut bled profusely, and he held a tissue against it, half turned from her as if he feared she would cut him again. The tissue grew bright red with blood. The cut itself was almost invisible but, he said, painful, and it bled off and on all morning. He was still wearing a little scrap of toilet paper over it when the bell rang and Amy Rordam stood on the doorstep.

"I was driving past and I just thought I'd stop by to see how you both are and if there's something I might do for you."

She reeled this off as she must have rehearsed it, her eyes locked with Susan's, as if daring her to say anything that would make her more embarrassed than she already was.

"Come in, come in," Susan said, holding the door open. Amy entered under her arm and Susan called into the house, "Fred, look who's here!"

He wheeled into the kitchen and thank God he had a smile on his face, but Amy was a good deal more relieved than she was.

"My, aren't you cheerful this morning, Frederick."

"He's been that way ever since he fell out of the bathtub two days ago."

"Fell out of the bathtub!" Amy covered her mouth with her hand, excited and embarrassed by Susan's remark.

"She left me alone in there. For hours."

"Isn't he awful, Amy? Can't even take a bath by himself."

"It gives her a thrill," Fred said in a fake whisper, winking at Amy.

"What's that on your nose?"

He remembered the bloody tissue still stuck to the nick in his nose. "I've been donating blood."

Amy turned her head to one side and looked at him from the corner of her eye.

"For some recipe of Susan's," he went on. "Are you staying for lunch?"

"Fred!"

Amy put the paper sack she was carrying on the table and pulled a plate of cookies covered with plastic wrap from it.

"Chocolate chip," she said.

Fred reacted like a boy, grabbing Amy's hand and kissing it with mock gallantry before wheeling within reach of the cookies. Susan got them before he did.

"Not in the middle of the morning," she said. "Remember what Doctor Carey said."

"That jerk. I think his tapeworm has a tapeworm. Let me have just one."

"After lunch."

"Just one."

It was Amy who relented, taking the dish from Susan and peeling back the plastic and handing a cookie to Fred.

"While they're still warm," she said.

"Like me."

"Fred!"

"I meant alive."

"Quit bragging," Susan said, and went out into the yard. It was her first chance in days to get away from him, and she didn't intend to miss it.

Fifteen minutes later from the back of the yard Susan looked up from her gardening. The screen door opened and Amy appeared. Was she going already? But then Fred came into view, on crutches, moving along slowly but surely. Once outside, he propped himself on the crutches and looked around as if surveying his property with an approving eye. Susan kept on working in the garden, but looking from under the brim of her sun hat at Fred and Amy. What a tonic it was for Fred, having someone his own age to show off for. Susan could kick herself for not asking Amy over before this. Whenever she suggested it, Fred went up in smoke, but look at him now. He would never do anything for her, she babied him too much. Besides, it was a kind of revenge, making her wait on him hand and foot. Poor Amy obviously got a thrill out of fussing over Fred, and he in turn was less of a burden. Dear God, wouldn't it be wonderful if those two had a sunset romance, married, and Fred was taken off her hands once and for all?

He came halfway down the yard on his crutches, with Amy at his side, and Susan rose and walked to them.

"Stay in the yard," she said.

"I thought we'd go for a ride." He said it with a straight face, as if he led a normal and nomadic life.

"Not now, Fred, I can't."

"I meant me and Amy."

"Only if you promise to keep him, Amy."

"Susan, he's kidding."

"That's what I used to think."

Amy's giggle was constant now, starting up just a little too late to be genuine.

Fred stayed on crutches until Amy left and then belted himself into his chair and gripped its arms as if he intended never to leave it again.

"You overdid."

"I did it. That's what bothers you."

"Fred, everything you do bothers me."

"Good."

5

ENCOURAGED BY Hilliard, Will Tonsor persevered in his pursuit of Amy Rordam.

"No, I do not golf," she said, scarcely opening her mouth to speak. He had waylaid her at the library, correctly guessing that she got a new supply of mysteries every other day.

"You could come along in the cart, you wouldn't have to golf."

"Will Tonsor, if you want a chauffeur or a caddy, you have come to the wrong person."

"It's not a chauffeur or caddy I want." Be bold, Hilliard had urged. Women expect the man to break the ice.

"What is that supposed to mean?" He felt as a worm must feel when looked at by a robin.

"I wasn't being suggestive."

"Just obtuse?"

He wasn't sure what that meant. Amy was a well-read

woman, cultivated. The librarian had told Will that Amy had read through the whole of the works of Agatha Christie twice. He did not ask how many books that was. If the librarian was impressed, who was he to quibble? Brenda Bowles, the librarian, was eager to please, a plump little woman in a polka dot dress whose neckline showed the tops of her comfortable breasts. Was Amy well endowed? She was small, anyway, and that's what he liked, no taller than Brenda. Brenda's left breast tilted her nameplate so he could read it easily. Her eyes twinkled receptively. If he had trusted his own judgment he would have transferred his affection from Amy to Brenda, but Hilliard insisted he was making progress. If that was true, Will hated to think what bombing out would be like.

"How about tennis?"

"Will Tonsor, I haven't an athletic bone in my body."

The remark seemed to invite his inspection, but she turned away with an indignant sound. She was four paces from him when she sailed a goodbye over her shoulder. Will turned to see Brenda looking out the library window. It was all he could do not to go inside and take advantage of the sympathy that shone in her eyes. But the memory of Matt Hilliard's encouragement stopped him. He raised his hand to wave, but Brenda had disappeared.

He started off with a jogging motion, then stopped himself; he wasn't dressed for exercise. Besides, he had already done his run for the day. He had felt in the pink—youthful, desirable—when he came here to find Amy. What the hell did turn Amy on? Who would know? The only person he could think of was Susan Nebens.

6

THE FOLLOWING day Fred was due for an appointment with Doctor Carey.

"Don't tell him about the crutches."

"You tell him."

"No. Let him think I'm atrophying."

Susan shrugged. Did he really think the doctor much cared one way or the other? The worst thing about Fred's self-centeredness was that it drew Susan's attention to her own. How can anyone help but be the center of his or her own world? But it was different with Fred, far different. He referred everything and everyone to himself.

"I'll get the car."

She would back out to the side of the house where it would be a lot easier getting him into the passenger seat. The car was used so seldom it started with difficulty, and Susan sat watching the gas needle rise slowly to indicate the tank was full. She always kept a full tank of gas in the station wagon. Harry had loved this car. It was big and noisy and consumed fuel ravenously, but Susan meant to drive it until it fell apart. She shifted into reverse and backed swiftly out of the garage, not wanting Fred to be in a snit from waiting.

She felt the thump before she heard the cry and a millisecond went by before she put on the brakes. She turned in the seat, but there was nothing to see. She began to get out of the car before putting it in neutral. It started to roll again and once more she heard the agonized cry. Fred! Outside the car she crouched and looked beneath. The right rear wheel was resting on him, just below his chest. His eyes rolled toward her, glistening with hatred, but even as she looked they dulled and the light went out of them.

Susan scrambled back into the car, put it in gear and eased it gently forward, continuing for six feet before stopping and jumping out again. Fred lay motionless on the drive now; his midsection and lower chest were sunken horribly. Even before she sought his pulse and put her ear to his chest, Susan knew that he was dead.

"There, there," she said aloud, as if reassuring both Fred and anyone else who might think he was dead. She cradled the broken body in her arms, then carried it, stooped over and very swiftly, into the garage where she laid it upon the stacks of newspapers he insisted she save. She needed a minute to think.

What in God's name should she do? There was a look of great concentration on Fred's face, as if he were trying to help. She lay her hand on his leathery skin and felt an awkward tenderness. "I'm sorry," she whispered. "You should have waited until I drove out." But of course from above he would know now whether it was her fault or his. He should have stayed in the house. Showing off with those crutches! She looked out and saw one crutch lying under the car and another on the driveway where it must have fallen. She scampered from the garage, picked up the crutches and put them in the back seat of the car to get them out of sight, then went back to Fred and explained to him that if she drove him to emergency they would simply pronounce him dead, and that was something she and Fred already knew. It helped to think of Fred's death as merely an event of the day, something they could quarrel about. And of course at the hospital there would be questions. All those forms and buxom misanthropic nurses who loved to put questions to you in bored tones, scribbling things down, their manner suggesting that whatever had happened was your fault. Well, no one in their right mind would think it was her fault that Fred had come outside as he never had before, that he had been standing there when she backed out of the garage just so it would be that much more convenient for him.

"You can see the pain in his face when he uses the crutches," Amy had said. "If I were you I'd hide them."

No point in telling Amy those grimaces were for her benefit. Agile athlete of seventy-five doing gymnastic tricks with only a pair of crutches, no net. No gain either. Had Fred led Amy to believe that he used the crutches frequently? Well, Amy got the credit for that. God knows Fred hadn't paid any attention to what Doctor Carey said.

Doctor Carey. The appointment! She pulled back the sleeve of her coat but couldn't make out the face of her watch. She extended her wrist into the sunlight, squinting

PART TWO

1

INSIDE THE house, Susan picked up the phone, closed her eyes and dialed the number from memory. She had even practiced dialing it in the dark, at night, in case the power ever went off, troubling only Doctor Carey's answering machine which told her when he would be in in the morning and a number she might call if this were an emergency. It was Grace Farber who answered the phone now.

"Grace, this is Susan Nebens. Fred has an appointment this afternoon . . ."

"In two minutes! Why aren't you here?"

Grace was three years younger than Susan, but she had her mother's schoolteacher manner and could fill anyone with guilt by the mere tone of her voice. She had her mother's massive bosom too, and when she leaned forward it lay on the reception desk like an undelivered baby.

"I know."

"Well, why aren't you here?"

"Isn't Fred there?" she asked wildly.

"How could he be if you haven't brought him?"

"You mean he's not there?" Susan did a passable imitation of Grace's mother as she asked the question.

"No, he isn't here."

"And I thought he meant to surprise me."

"Are you saying you don't know where he is?"

"Grace, he knows about the appointment, he is a grown man and either he will show up or he won't." And she slammed down the phone on a note of satisfaction. The fact that she was lying did not diminish her sense of having scored against Grace.

Five minutes later the doorbell rang and Susan peeked out to see Amy Rordam standing there, trying to be nonchalant. She appeared to be trying on various expressions she might use when the door was answered. When Susan did open the door, Amy had chosen a little frown that went with the half smile on her pursed lips.

"Susan, is Fred here?"

"He had an appointment with Doctor Carey at two."

The frown deepened. "Back so soon?"

"I never went and now I'm worried. I just talked with Doctor Carey's office and they haven't seen him either."

"Haven't seen him! But could he just go off by himself?"

"It's those darned crutches."

Amy's mouth remained ajar. "But how far could he go alone on those?"

She asked Amy in and offered to make tea, a mistake; Amy shook the suggestion away as not befitting this anxious moment. It helped to have Fred's absence a problem she shared with Amy and Doctor Carey's office; she could almost forget the awful noise the car had made when it struck Fred and his high, protesting voice as life was leaving him. Susan refused to think of Fred lying in the garage on top of those stacks of newspapers. It was too grotesque to be true. The dead body of an old man lying on a pile of well-wrapped trash in a closed garage, his rib cage crushed.

"You saw him the other day, Amy."

"That's what I mean. It was agony for him to get about on those things."

"Amy, sometimes Fred makes things seem just a little worse than they were."

"Did he?" Amy drew back from this heretical statement and looked at Susan the way Grace Farber's mother always had.

"I think once in a while he deserves a chance to complain a bit." At the moment, Susan was more than willing to make the concession.

"He didn't complain to me."

"He is very good about his crutches."

Susan listened to herself in disbelief. What in the name of God was she doing? No matter what she said to Grace and Amy, Fred was in the garage on top of those stacks of newspapers, dead, and nothing could change that. But it was the thought of the crutches in the back seat of the car that bothered her more. How could she explain not taking Fred to Doctor Carey's if the crutches were still here.

"Well, I can't just sit here, Amy. I'm going to Doctor Carey's office and see if he showed up."

"Why don't you just telephone?"

And talk to Grace again? "He could be anywhere between here and there."

Amy just shook her head. "Susan, that doesn't make sense. Good as he might have been with the crutches, he couldn't go off downtown by himself."

"That's what bothers me."

"When did you realize he was missing?"

"When he didn't show up for lunch."

"Had you seen him this morning?"

"Of course. I made his breakfast, then he watched television." Would Amy approve of what Fred had enjoyed on daytime television, the most insipid audience-participation shows, various trios reading news in their studios? But Susan had the feeling Amy would forgive Fred anything. After all, the man had suffered so bravely.

"If you go, I'll stay here."

"Why!"

"Why? What if he comes back here instead of to the doctor's office?" Amy made a face and shook her head. "I just can't believe he went away by himself."

"There's no need for you to stay here, Amy." She could drive off with the crutches in the car, but leaving Amy in the house with Fred lying dead in the garage was out of the question. Next to the back door was the remote-control device for opening and closing the garage door, but the station wagon still stood in the driveway. Susan deactivated the remote control. "Come along with me, Amy."

"But what if he comes back?"

"He won't. I'm sure of it."

That made no sense, but Amy found it convincing. She was prepared to believe anything about Fred. Poor thing, Susan thought, had she been daydreaming about herself and Fred these past days? And then just showing up on the doorstep unannounced. If she had come half an hour earlier, the whole world might have been different, but no matter. Susan had hit upon the solution.

"Amy, I wonder if he hobbled over to your place."

"Why would he do a thing like that?" But the smile burst through her attempt to frown.

"You go right home and call me as soon as you get there."

Amy nodded at the manifest good sense of this. "I'll call," she said, on the way to the door. But she stopped and impulsively hugged Susan, and then she was gone.

2

SUSAN WATCHED Amy hurry down the drive to her little car, buckle herself in and pull away in haste. But before she herself could leave the house the phone rang.

"Susan Nebens? Will Tonsor. How's everything with you?"

He spoke with the breezy intrusiveness of a salesman, and that is what he had been.

"Fred's not here, Will."

"Lucky you. Susan, I want to pick your brain."

Susan closed her eyes in an agony of impatience. She had to get rid of those crutches.

"It's about Amy Rordam."

"Amy!"

"Now, don't be shocked. I like Amy and I'd like to know her better and I'm asking you to do a little matchmaking."

Susan listened to disbelief. Will's exercising had the effect of making him look older, cadaverous, fragile. She remembered him in his jogging outfit, looking like someone just released from the Gulag. On the one hand, she admired him for staying active; on the other, she thought he overdid it. And now asking about Amy?

"Unless of course there'd be a conflict of interest," Will added, chuckling.

"How do you mean?"

"I thought maybe Fred had his eye on her."

"Fred? Oh, no." And then, shamelessly, she decided to put this silly request to good use. "As a matter of fact, I think you may find Amy very receptive. She just left here."

"Why do you think so?"

"That she'd be interested? Call it a woman's intuition. You should find her at home. I'm going to have to run, Will."

"Wish me luck!"

Outside, Susan hopped into the station wagon and was off with a speed exceeding Amy's. Where was she going? She actually had to think before she remembered she meant to get rid of the crutches. Her story was that Fred must have gone off on his own, using his crutches, so she had to get them out of the station wagon. Where? She waited, frowning, for a light to change and then an idea vaguely teased her mind, along with fugitive memories of *The Song of Bernadette.* Ten minutes later she was parked on the street outside St. Anthony's church. The unstated logic of this objective did not dawn on her until she was on her way up the steps to the main entrance, a crutch in either hand, as if she were demonstrating her ability to walk without them. Lourdes, Ste Anne de Beaupré, other places, Catholics had been way ahead of Oral Roberts and that bunch, believing in cures from drinking holy water and going to where the

Blessed Virgin appeared. Susan had been in Catholic churches only twice in her life, for weddings, and never in St. Anthony's, but this was the largest Catholic church in town, a more likely place for a miracle to occur than St. Boniface's or Our Lady of Mercy. The doors were massive and looked locked, but they gave way under the pressure of her shoulder. The vestibule was surprisingly small, crowded with racks and display cases of religious literature, the parish bulletin, *Crisis* and other churchy magazines.

The inner doors swung open like those of a saloon in a TV western, and Susan peeked in. There was a woman at the altar doing something with candles, and two-thirds of the way up the aisle an old man sat, his hair wild on his head. He stared at the altar, either praying or watching what the woman was doing. For a crazy moment, Susan thought it might be Fred. He had prayed for a cure and now sat gratefully talking to God. The woman got a new candle into a holder and Susan slipped inside the church, the crutches held behind her. Neither the woman nor the old man noticed her. There was a side altar on the left with a statue that looked like Saint Francis holding a baby. Susan went closer, propped the crutches against the railing that enclosed the shrine and hurried out of the church. In the vestibule, taking advantage of the slowing swing of the doors, she looked back and saw that neither the old man nor woman at the altar had paid any attention to her. She felt almost lighthearted as she drove home to the dead body of Fred in the garage.

She knew now what she was going to do. When she said those things to Grace and Amy, she had thought she was losing her mind. Maybe she was in a state of shock after what happened. The point of everything she said was to deflect the remotest hint of accusation from herself. Backing over Fred had been an accident pure and simple; she knew that. The truth ought to be all a person needed, but in her secret heart Susan heard the accusations. Hadn't she often dreamt of how nice her life would be after Fred was gone? What if her desire had made her careless and running over Fred, while it looked like an accident, really represented her heart's desire? She could imagine some smirking lawyer developing this for the jury, twelve resentful fellow citizens who looked forward to putting Susan away. Why should she have all her late husband's money when she couldn't even take care of his father, for heaven's sake? Susan dreaded the prospect of private, let alone public, discussion of her life with Fred. Everyone said how good she was with him, but Susan had made her share of such statements and knew what they were worth. People said what they thought the caretaker wanted to hear. Hadn't she always hinted that her life was a kind of martyrdom? Why else would so many people have told her it was?

The phone sounded as if it had been ringing for a long time when she came in and picked it up.

"Susan! Is he there?"

"I was just going to ask you the same question, Grace."

"Where've you been? I've been trying to reach you."

"Out checking some of his favorite places."

"Fred's?"

"He liked the courthouse, particularly if there was a trial. And churches."

"Are we talking about the same old bastard?"

"Grace!"

"I quote the man himself. That is what he told me to put down when I asked him what his profession was or had been."

"It doesn't sound as bad when he says it."

"It does to me. Hold for Doctor Carey."

Abruptly music erupted in her ear. Susan held the instrument from her head but could still hear the insipid strains. She lay the phone on the counter.

The music stopped and Doctor Carey began to speak. "I've got Earl's X-rays here and I'm sorry to say there's no fracture."

"Doctor . . ."

"Fractures are easier, is what I mean. What we have here is a lot of torn cartilage."

"This is Susan Nebens, Doctor Carey. My father-in-law, Fred, missed his appointment this afternoon."

A pause. "What's the matter, was he sick?" He wheezed in what might have been an imitation of Fred but was Doctor Carey's excuse for a laugh.

"He's missing."

"How so?"

"I don't know where he is. I thought maybe he'd gone to your office on his own."

"Fred?"

"He's been practicing with his crutches a lot lately. I thought maybe he wanted to impress you."

"Hasn't he been using them all along?"

Did he even remember who Fred was? He had Earl's X-rays, whoever Earl was, rather than Fred's folder. Did he know who anyone was without their folder?

"Where was he?"

"I still don't know. He's not back."

"Okay. Well, let me know. We'll set up another appointment. Talk to Grace. Things are so busy here I didn't even notice he didn't show."

The music began again and Susan put down the phone.

3

AMY ANSWERED her phone breathlessly, perhaps thinking it was Fred.

"Amy! Will Tonsor."

"What on earth do you want?"

"Just a little tender loving care."

"What!"

"Now stop being coy, Amy. People have told me you like me, so there's no need to pretend."

"What people?"

"Does it really matter?"

"It matters to me. You've been misinformed, Will Tonsor. And you call at a particularly bad time. Fred Nebens is missing . . ."

"Fred? Missing is right. He's a few cards short of a full deck."

"Will, goodbye."

She did not slam down the phone, although that is what she wanted to do. She was furious at the effontery of Will Tonsor. He must have been drinking. Probably sitting around the bar at the country club. Well, he had nothing better to do. Except to run around the streets half clothed. Honestly. Amy could remember a better time when a man would have been arrested for appearing in public dressed like that.

Why did she so instinctively resist his advances? Because old as he was he still cast himself in the role of protector, as if he were her father. Memories of her father caused little more than pain. How could she feel tender about a man who led his family such a hellish life? Not that his times of intemperance were frequent. Her mother had once calculated that they represented less than one percent of their life together. But it could happen at any time. Each day could be the day when Ole Rordam fell, walked into a bar from which he would not emerge until he was thoroughly drunk. He stayed drunk for days, usually a week, emerging from the bout haggard and filled with self-hatred. How can you lean on someone who is liable to fall over without warning?

Amy preferred the already weakened Fred. He did not raise one's expectations. She would not rely on him, he would rely on her. But these, she scolded herself, were foolish thoughts. She was carrying on like a girl. Did she really think that her life might change? Did she believe that now, at this time in her life, she would do what she had thus far failed to do, link her life with a man's? The odd thing was that it seemed less risky now. For one thing, it did not threaten an endless future. And of course the physical side would be less important. Or was that true of Will Tonsor? Maybe that is why she preferred Fred.

The phone began to ring again and she glared at it, but it went right on ringing. She picked it up and, eyes closed, put it to her ear.

4

"STILL NO sign of him, Amy," Susan said into the phone.

She had returned from her quick trip downtown with a sense of accomplishment. She left the station wagon in the drive when the garage door did not respond to the remote control, came inside and immediately dialed Amy Rordam's number.

"Have you informed the police?" Amy's voice was high and unnatural.

"I am giving him one more hour."

"Why?"

"It's just a little bargain I made. Can you imagine how silly I'd look if I reported him missing and he shows up in a cab?"

"Cabs! Of course. Have you checked the cab companies?"

"Amy, would you do that for me?"

With Amy taken care of, Susan checked the street out

front and the neighboring houses before reactivating the remote control and lifting the garage door. Fred lay where she
had left him, frowning into eternity. She averted her face
and put her arms under him and then wondered how wise
it was to carry him out to the car. And she hadn't opened
the car door. Did she intend to put him on the ground,
open the door, pick him up again? She began to laugh. It
was funny, she insisted, not quite daring to look at Fred's
disapproving expression, but a part of her agreed with him.
Was she crazy, laughing about carrying a dead body
around?

She stood in the open door of the garage, hugging herself
for a moment until she remembered that her arms had just
been cradling the dead body of Fred. It was time she spoke
some sense to herself. What on earth was she doing? Her
plan had been to take the body downtown, a block or so
from St. Anthony's, and leave it in the street. It would be
thought that he had died from being run over by a car.
There would be a search for the hit-and-run driver and Susan
could breathe in peace, free from stated and unstated criti-
cisms of the way she had taken care of Harry's father.

The sight of her dead father-in-law would not permit her
to carry out this crazy plan. Now her trip downtown with
the crutches seemed a product of her imagination, not something she had actually done. She had to start acting sensibly,
call the police and explain what had happened. *I was backing
out of the garage to take my father-in-law to the doctor, and
somehow he got out of the house without help and was in the
path of the car. I hit him without any idea he was there. He
never came outside alone. By the time I could stop it was too
late.* At which point, Fred's body would be inspected and
everyone would see there was nothing she could have done.

Why hadn't she called the police immediately? Or an ambulance?

Why had she lied to Grace and Doctor Carey?

Why had she pretended to Amy Rordam that Fred might have gone to the doctor on his own?

Even answering those questions, difficult as that might prove to be, was better than going on with the pretense that Fred had somehow disappeared.

A car door slammed and the stick figure of Amy Rordam appeared, bustling up the driveway. Susan pressed the button and stepped out of the garage as the door began to descend. It went down slowly, with many groans and complaints, and Amy was moving at twice her normal pace. Susan stood frozen by the garage, as if to prevent Amy from bending down and catching a glimpse of Fred before the door closed completely.

"I called all three cab companies and none of them gave him a ride."

"Thanks for taking care of that, Amy."

"Oh, I'm not done. There are the independents."

Susan nodded. "That would be like Fred. He hated organizations and companies and groups." It was why he had remained a barber, or so Harry had said. Susan wondered if Fred had the talent for anything else. In any case, he enjoyed the fierce independence of running his own shop, pontificating behind the chair where he had the customer at his mercy. Barbering was not the same profession he had entered by the time he closed his shop. Fewer men got haircuts, and those who did wanted to be styled rather than cut. Fred had viewed these developments with disgust rather than alarm. But in the end, he too resorted to shears and blow dryers and haircuts meant to look as if they hadn't happened. The old ways weren't a matter of principle with him. What he wanted was an ear into which to pour his theories and judgments on the passing scene. He had been a close student of the newspaper in those days, a faithful listener to the news. The all-news station from Chicago, WBBM, which extended its reach into neighboring states, was always on in the shop, providing constant topics for interpretation. This idyl had been threatened several times by attempts to organize independent barbers.

"Organized independents!" Fred had fumed. "What the hell is that supposed to mean?"

It meant leaning on the suppliers to provide talcs and towels and shampoos and the rest at lower prices. Fred would have none of it. What if customers organized to force him to drive down his prices?

Telling Amy all this in the kitchen, putting on the coffee, Susan felt how odd it was to be talking about him here in the house he had haunted for these past years. But those were the years when she had told no one what it was really like to live with Fred. Not that she was criticizing him now. Besides, Amy was interested in anything Susan had to say about Fred. It seemed cruel to feed that curiosity, with Fred in the garage on top of those piles of papers, but Susan needed the neutralizing effect of speaking of Fred as if he were still among the living. As she poured the coffee, ceding to Amy's detailed recital of her telephoning the cab companies, Susan realized how risky it would be to drive off in daylight with Fred laid out in the back seat. Imagine stopping at a light and having pedestrians look in at him. Of course they would think he was napping. Or drunk. The thought was prompted by Amy's discreet question.

"Fred isn't a drinker, is he, Susan?"

"Why would you ask a thing like that?"

Amy's glasses flashed with the setting sun as she turned away and Susan remembered. Amy's father had been an alcoholic, going months, sometimes a year, without a drink and then all of a sudden off on a toot that lasted for days and days, undoing everything he had accomplished. Amy had lived her life like someone in the shadow of Vesuvius, lulled into optimism and then suddenly, without warning, the eruption.

"Did he?"

But she could not bring herself to tell that lie about Fred. She shook her head. "It made him sick."

"It makes anyone sick." Amy's rounded eyes sought Susan's. "It is a sickness."

Alcoholism was invented to make it easier on the drunk, but mainly it helps the family. One of Fred's pronouncements, occasioned by talk of Ole Rordam. *Everything's a sickness now. If you rob banks, it's not your fault. Kill a dozen people, there's something wrong with your psyche. It's gotten so nobody can do anything wrong.* Fred's voice had risen as he said this. Clearly, doing something wrong, consciously, deliberately, was an inalienable right and he would fight for it. Or at least talk for it.

"I think Will Tonsor drinks," Amy said.

"What makes you think so?"

"It's a long story."

Susan wished Amy had not come back. It was unnerving to have the little woman actually expecting to see Fred alive. What would Amy say if she knew Fred lay dead on a stack of newspapers in the garage?

"I'll stay here with you if you like, Susan."

"Nonsense. There's nothing to do."

"Waiting can be harder than anything else. Call the police, Susan. There's no point in putting it off."

"Amy, there's something else."

"What?"

"His crutches are missing. I should have checked that right away."

A small, sad smile spread over Amy's plain face. "Susan, you're not making sense. Of course his crutches are missing. How else could he have left?"

"You're right."

"And if he was capable of walking off on crutches, you can be sure that nothing has happened to him."

Amy smiled reassuringly and Susan felt a wave of sadness for her. Did Amy imagine that Fred would come back and show interest in her?

"We must notify the police, Susan."

"I just can't bring myself to do it."

"I understand." Amy picked up the phone. "I'll make the call."

Susan went to the bathroom where she studied her face in the mirror, looking for telltale signs of the dreadful thing she had done to Fred and the worse things she had done since. Amy was still on the phone when she returned to the kitchen.

"They want us to go down there," Amy said, shocked.

"Not tonight."

Into the phone, Amy said, "If you can't come here, we can do it by telephone." She covered the phone as she listened, then whispered, "They want a photograph."

Where was she going to find a photograph of Fred that looked like the old man he had become? He had refused to have his picture taken for years, turned away or covered his face, as if he were a spy or a celebrity. Not that it mattered.

"He is on crutches," Amy said into the phone, speaking with such authority that Susan almost believed it was true.

PART THREE

1

PAUL ARTHUR Morley had joined the Belting police force for the pension. Twenty years of boring duty, then retire, draw the pension and take another job, that was the idea, but he had been a cop now for thirty-five years and almost wished it was more dangerous than it was so he could count on dying with his boots on. But he had never suffered a scratch in the line of duty. Any attraction retirement had held for him had long since faded before the specter of those who had done what he himself had planned to do. As soon as they had the second job, they started talking about another retirement plan, plus social security. The good life always lay in the future. Retirement was a dream, like the Muhammedan heaven, milk and honey and dancing girls. A vacation was all right because you knew it wouldn't last. He and Ginny spent a week in Sarasota every February, soaking up some sun and visiting with Vic and Martha

Chase. Paul had ridden patrol with Vic when he himself was a rookie and Vic was already within reach of the pension. He got it and moved to Florida and took an ad in the yellow pages as a general handyman, jack of all trades, any job the big boys wouldn't handle. He always cleared the dates the Morleys would be down so they would see Florida to its best advantage. Paul had come to doubt that their week together was typical of the life Vic and Martha led in Sarasota.

"All she talks about is people back home," Ginny said, curled against his back in the motel double bed. At home they slept in twin beds. It was a relief the two women were talking. The year before Martha had accused Ginny of flirting with Vic, which was true, but she was just paying Paul back.

"So she misses them."

"That's what I'm saying."

"Sounds natural enough."

"Paul, she's lonesome."

Everybody was lonesome some of the time, for one thing or another. Anyway, he already suspected life was not as Vic and Martha had imagined it would be, and he didn't want to talk about it. Once you start ticking off mistakes people made, where would it end? Including Paul Arthur and Ginny.

"Maybe if I'd tried to get a job on the Sarasota force . . ."

"God, I'm glad you didn't."

Yeah. At the time she had gone on a two-week silent treatment, punishing him for not even looking into the smartest idea he had ever had. It was Vic's idea, but Vic would have known that half the cops in the country are trying to move to Florida and California, same with postal employees. His chances had been lousy, even if he had been

interested, which he wasn't. When you build something, you
make sure you give water a way to run, to drain the property,
to carry the rain off the roof. The twin beds provided Ginny
with her run-off. They had weathered it and here she was
now telling him she was glad he hadn't done it. Well, he
might have screwed up their lives for good with the Widow
Brady. At the time, she had been Cleopatra, Wallace
Simpson, you name it, he would have killed for her. Fortunately, she could be had for a lot less. It wasn't just that he
let it burn out, she tired of him too, having found someone
willing to confer both his pension and his GI insurance on
her. Brady had died leaving her with her good looks and
nothing else. But there had been a week when Paul had
come very close to telling Ginny it was all over between
them. The kids? They would make it. The house? She could
have it. The summer place up on Lake Winnetka? Everything. He would give his immortal soul to spend his nights
in Irene Brady's bed. To this day, whenever he felt contempt
for the poor bastards who fell into the arms of the police,
he reminded himself of Irene Brady. Ginny too brought it
up from time to time. Moving to Florida was to remove him
from temptation, that was one of her arguments.

"I don't think Vic's business is going too good."

"Why do you say that?" She snuggled closer. Away from
home it was like sleeping with a stranger. Besides, nothing
brings a couple closer together than the bad news of friends.

"He never talks about it."

"What kind of reason is that?"

Probably the best. Vic took pride in doing well what he
did and if he were doing much he would have talked about
it. As it was, he sounded like a tour director. No wonder.
The day before they left he took Paul up to the St. Petersburg

dock where fishing boats for hire lined one wharf. GO FOR THE BIG ONES WITH CAP'N JACK. Cap'n Jack had grown up in landlocked Nebraska, joined the Navy as a kid and been on water ever since. They went up on the flying bridge and Jack showed them the controls, then turned a weathered look on the sun-spangled bay. "Big ones waiting out there today," he said.

On the wharf men with kids in tow wistfully read Cap'n Jack's brochure. "C'mon back without the wife and kids, mate. Let's go fishing."

"God, would I like to."

"Do it. That's how I got here."

There was a wife in Maui and several dusky kids, but Jack kept hearing the call of the sea.

"See you Monday, Vic." Cap'n Jack said.

"I help him out," Vic explained.

"Fishing?"

"Getting customers."

Paul could see Vic there on the wharf, urging tourists to go after the big ones. He wouldn't have gotten that tan doing odd jobs. Or maybe helping Cap'n Jack was just the oddest job of all.

When the week was up, Paul and Ginny fled northward with thanks in their hearts and Paul found on his desk the strange disappearance of Frederick Nebens. By this time, the old man's crutches had been found in St. Anthony's, and some woman named Rordam was announcing a miraculous cure.

"It's plain as day. He hobbled into church in desperation and walked out a well man, leaving his crutches behind."

"I saw that show on television. Father Dowling."

She looked at him over her glasses. "St. Anthony is a miracle worker."

The crutches did belong to Fred, although his daughter-in-law was not eager to identify them, let alone claim a miraculous cure. Amy Rordam had no idea where a cured Fred might have gone.

"I would have thought he'd go to Amy first of all," Susan Nebens said. Paul wished she wouldn't encourage her friend that way.

"Fred related to Harry Nebens?"

"Did you know him?"

"Something happen to him?"

Susan inhaled through her nose, eyes closed. Amy said, "He's dead." She leaned toward him as she said this.

"He was my husband."

"No kidding. I know him. Knew him. Calhoun High."

"What year did you graduate?"

He had been in the class ahead of Harry, they had played baseball together, he hadn't seen him since. The widow perked up at this and the Widow Brady warning went off in his head. "Harry was my age."

She nodded. She wanted him to say it. What the hell. He said it.

"You're a lot younger than Harry."

"Well, younger."

"Who would have thought his old man was still alive?"

Amy Rordam didn't like that. "For all we know, he isn't, and I don't see that very much is being done about it."

"I thought I'd find out what the problem is before I solve it, ma'am."

"Susan and I have been doing little else but explaining what happened since it happened."

"I've been on vacation."

"Where?" Susan asked.

"We like Florida. Sarasota."

"Harry always dreamt of going there. When he retired."

Paul thought of boats lying upside down on the Florida beaches, their hulls baking in the sun, waiting, waiting. He thought of marinas where the masts of boats swayed in the wind. He thought of Vic and Cap'n Jack. Other places fascinate. Like other women.

"Thank God for his pension," Paul said.

"I'd rather have Harry."

"And you got the old man instead?"

Amy Rordam interrupted, "We would like to get him back."

"You got a recent photograph of your father-in-law?"

Susan thought about it, adopting a cute puzzled expression. Paul Morley bet she had no idea how cute she looked. "Not a recent one."

"He didn't change much with age," the Rordam woman said.

"We got him down as a missing person. I mean Fred."

"He has been missing two days." Amy Rordam seemed to think the police should know where everyone was at all times. "How long does it usually take to find someone?"

No point in telling her that many missing persons stayed missing. For that matter, most murders went unsolved or at least unpunished. "It varies."

"He is an old man. He can't really take care of himself."

"Even with the miraculous cure?"

That shut her up. The daughter-in-law, Harry Nebens's widow, had little to say. Maybe she was sick and tired of talking about it. Maybe she understood that the likelihood of finding the old man at all, let alone alive, was on the order of, well, a miracle. It was because she didn't nag that Paul resolved to give the case his best shot.

And that was before Amanda Tracy, Chicago lady journalist, decided to make a crusade of Frederick Nebens.

2

TALKING TO Lieutenant Morley about Fred, Susan was viv-
idly reminded of Harry. As Paul Morley said, he and Harry
had been more or less the same age.

She said little. In the circumstances, her usual remarks
about finding Fred no burden at all seemed out of place.
Nor did she want to tell Paul Morley that caring for Fred
was like doing something for Harry, it kept him alive in her
heart. His question about the pension had an edge to it,
until he remembered Fred.

"I don't like him," Amy said.

"Why?"

"He has no sense of urgency. You'd think he'd come on
a social visit. Doesn't he realize that Fred is out there somewhere, wandering around, lost?"

Did Amy really believe that? Well, she said she believed
that Fred had been cured in St. Anthony's, that he had

thrown down his crutches like the man in the Bible and gone dancing into the street. A thoughtful look came over Amy's round face when it occurred to her that a miracle that restored him to health so he could dance into oblivion was not the kind you prayed for. If you were Amy. Not that Susan would have prayed for such a thing to happen, but then she didn't believe in miracles anyway.

"Do you think he'll be found?" Susan asked him when she was letting him out the front door.

"We can only hope."

"He was old and feeble. I can't imagine him surviving." She shuddered as she had shuddered that morning when she looked out and saw two scrawny dogs sniffing around the trash she had taken down to the curb. She had been powerfully tempted to put Fred down there too, but the thought of the bag splitting open, or the trashman becoming curious, stopped her. She sailed out of the house, shouting at the dogs. They looked at her over their shoulders as if wondering what she would do next. She kept on coming and they loped off, looking back at her. Susan was waving her arms, conscious that she would be a spectacle to any neighbor who looked out. Perhaps they would think she had earned the right to act a little flaky, considering what she was going through. They didn't know the half of it. She might have been shooing those dogs away from a trash bag containing Fred.

It was a good thing she was alone when she first noticed an odd odor coming from the garage. Grass cuttings? She let herself in and lowered the door and there was no doubt it was Fred.

Susan took one of the large plastic bags, half full of grass clippings, and rolled Fred into it. When she first put him atop the stack of newspapers, she had tucked up his arms and legs, so he wouldn't be conspicuous, and now it would have been hard to straighten him out. But it made getting him into the plastic bag easier. She closed the top and sealed it with a twist of plastic-enclosed wire and for the first time since she had looked under the car and seen his malevolent still-living eye look back at her, Susan felt free of Fred.

But what was she going to do with him? She thought again of leaving him in the street, but given the condition of the body, doubt would be cast on whether he had just been lying there since being struck. She already had enough questions she didn't want to answer and did not want to add to them. It would be far better if Fred were never found, as if one day he had wandered off when she wasn't looking and was never seen again. One of life's mysteries. The newspapers are full of them, as Fred would have been the first to attest. Except he had been extremely skeptical about missing persons.

"A guy paying alimony, you know he just took off. I say that's the explanation nine times out of ten."

"Alimony?"

"Escape. Wanting to start over. It's a waste of taxpayers' money to try finding them. It would be different if they ever succeeded."

Fred turned out to be an exception to his own theory, but nonetheless Susan felt she had his blessing. One of his favorite subjects had been his own funeral, his desire not to have one. A pine box and a hole in the ground were good enough for him. Or better, cremation. All the rest was crap anyway, crocodile tears before rummaging through what the deceased had left.

"You're awful."

"It's true."

He loved it when he thought he was shocking her. His mouth would widen in a wicked grin, and his lips would part to reveal that ridiculous denture, his uppers looking like a toothpaste ad misplaced in his wizened head.

She waited until it was dark. It was hard getting him into the back seat, because the body just wouldn't give at all anymore, so she flattened out the seat and slid him in from the back. She drove at a slow speed, out of respect. After all, this was Fred's last ride. He hadn't wanted a big funeral, but not even Fred would have imagined anything as minimal as this, so she would make it up to him in respect and dignity. There wasn't much she could do about potholes, of course, nor the railroad tracks she had to cross to get to the mall on the south side of town. She had decided what she would do with him. Her destination was the big yellow dumpster in the parking lot of the mall.

She entered the lot and tried to drive at ten m.p.h. or less, but an impatient horn behind her kept her moving. Her plan was to park as close to the dumpster as she could and, when the opportunity presented itself, to get Fred into it, plastic bag and all. The lot was poorly lit, which was a plus, but she had to make a circuit of it several times before finding a place within easy reach of the dumpster. Friday night, people doing their big shopping on payday—she seriously wondered if now was the time to do this. But she was here and she was anxious to have it over with. She couldn't sleep knowing Fred was out there in the garage, scrunched into the fetal position, brittle. She had tried to shut his eyes, but the lids wouldn't move. She tried to keep out of range of his unseeing gaze. Susan had never been superstitious, but she understood now how people got that way. Out of guilt she could imagine that her first startled reaction when she looked under the car was imprinted on Fred's eyes, just as out of loneliness Amy could imagine a miraculously restored Fred traipsing over to her house with the good news.

Susan decided she would shop first, to put off her grim task. Wending her way through the parking lot from her car, she wished she wasn't parked so far away. Women were accosted in such circumstances. Imagine if Amy could see her walking among this sea of cars, unprotected, a prey for demented men. Joking about it helped some, but she was glad to be inside the bright, busy mall, shoppers drifting along wearing the expression of good consumers, willing to be persuaded by claims of 10, 20, even 40 percent off. Off what? Bathing Suits Half Off. One of Fred's little jokes. She had taken him to this mall once or twice and he had hated it. The sight of other old people like himself dutifully walking from end to end mightily, clad in their brightly colored jogging suits, sickened him, or so he said.

"They trying out for the track team or what?"

"Just keeping limber."

"They look it, don't they?"

Balloonlike women puffed pinkly along, not quite sure of the ankle-high tennis shoes they wore. They did look silly. Or was she developing protection of her own? She should get more exercise herself.

The old people were not in evidence on Friday night, a night of serious shopping, stores crowded. They would get bowled over if they tried exercising now. Except for Will Tonsor, that is. Here he was wearing street clothes and moving through the crowd, a head taller than most others, beaming benevolently. His expression changed to exaggerated surprise when he saw Susan and began to wade toward her.

"Where's Fred?"

"Will, I'm worried sick. He's still missing. I haven't any idea where he is."

"Missing? Did you look under the beds? He can't get out of the house alone, can he?"

"Not easily."

"Say, did anything I said spur the old guy to stop acting as if he had one foot in the grave?"

"Something got into him. He's been showing off with his crutches."

"Showing off for whom?"

"Amy Roidam."

Will had crab-apple cheeks and a fine white mustache that Fred despised. Now he made it wobble and looked accusingly at Susan.

"You gave me a bum steer there, lady. Amy won't give me the time of day."

"Oh, I don't believe that." There was no point in Amy's mooning over Fred. She should be glad to have Will Tonsor interested in her.

"You think I should persist?"

"It makes the world go round, Will."

"Of course. That's probably what Fred is up to. Churchy la farm. Leave it to the French to have a phrase for it."

And off he went ho-hoing through the crowd, like an off-season Santa. And with him went all thought of leaving Fred in the dumpster in the parking lot. Of course Will would remember having seen her here, and she would be asked why she had gone there to look for Fred. The whole point of the mall had been to direct questions away from her, and now Will Tonsor had spoiled it.

She spent twenty minutes trying to find her car. Because

it took her that long to find the yellow dumpster. Only she couldn't find the station wagon. There were fewer cars in the mall now, and he heart was in her mouth as she walked into the shadowed, ill-lit area of the lot near the dumpster. Why hadn't she parked closer to the stores? She could have driven by the dumpster later. Fear for her own safety was replaced by another fear when the station wagon was not where she was sure she had left it. She wandered around until she finally admitted to herself that the station wagon was truly gone. My God, what was she going to do now?

She started back toward the stores, toward the warm, welcoming lights, her step quickening as she went. Her fear had changed to a feeling of total confusion. Someone had stolen the station wagon and driven away with the bag containing Fred's body. She wanted to think that the theft solved her problems, but her fear was that they were just beginning. Inside the mall again, she found a telephone and called a cab rather than the police, wanting to cultivate in privacy the sense that a great weight had been lifted from her.

PART FOUR

1

AMANDA TRACY'S father had died in Vietnam, releasing her mother for a series of marriages: she careened from Justice of the Peace to divorce court to the jag and/or fat farm and on to further romance. Amanda had rescued the home movies in which her father figured, most often giving instructions to whoever was holding the camera, and had them transferred to videotape so that she could put it on the VCR and shamelessly indulge the sense of having been abandoned as a child. There were orphans who had it better than she did, Amanda would bet on it, but of course it was not the sort of thing she talked about. The pitiable waif cast upon the sea of life as a preschooler, the child and young girl bereft of reliable adult guidance, the young woman who had the sense of speaking the commonplaces of human life as if they were part of a learned language, her native tongue a snarled dialect unintelligible to those who had a normal upbringing—that was the secret Amanda, unsuspected by those who encountered the self-assured, omnicompetent, obviously on-the-rise young writer for the *Sun-Times* whose current crusade was the unappreciated oldest generation of Americans. There were those among her Chicago colleagues who suspected that she was onto Pulitzer stuff here, the ideal combination of heart-wringing subject and accusative approach. Clearly *somebody* ought to be doing *something* about this, though who and how and where and other such questions were not of course the province of the journalist, the faithful recorder of the daily flow of events.

It was the hunch that her theme might find the vehicle for a story or two in the strange case of Frederick Nebens that had brought her to Belting. She would gamble her career, her hope of fortune and possibly fame to putting his plight and that of other elders before Chicago readers and the nation too, the stories being syndicated right from the start.

What does it mean to grow old in America? The case of Frederick Nebens could provide the materials for an answer to that question.

Is it possible for a man of 75, a man who uses crutches only with difficulty, to wander away from his home in a sizable American city and defy frantic efforts to locate him?

Can a man whose mind by all accounts was clear, whose disposition was positive, if not outrightly cheerful, disappear from the face of the earth, leaving no trace?

Alas, many things are possible given society's present feeble commitment to the growing number of elderly citi-

zens whose particular needs and proclivities represent a vast terra incognita to those still actively in the work force.

These and other far-ranging issues Amanda would use Fred's disappearance to address. The questions were general, but her approach would be resolutely singular.

"How much did he weigh?"

"Weigh?" The daughter-in-law tipped her head to one side and looked at Amanda from the corners of her eyes. Amanda waited. "Doctor Carey would know."

"But you don't?"

"I could guess."

Amanda waited. It was important to get off on the right foot and she wanted Susan on the defensive. Amanda had counted on gaining easy entrée to the daughter-in-law by appealing to the desire for publicity most people harbor, but also by being accusative. After all, this was the woman who had misplaced a man of seventy-five.

"One hundred forty?"

Amanda wrote it down, with the question mark.

"What size shoes did he wear?"

Susan had to go look.

Amanda went through it all, shirt size, length of trousers, then on to the physical characteristics, color of eyes, condition of teeth. Susan may have lived with and taken care of Frederick Nebens, but she had remarkable difficulty coming up with elementary facts about him.

"That isn't the way I knew him," Susan said plaintively.

"How did you know him?"

"Do you know the clothes size of your parents, their weight?"

Amanda would have, she bet on that. But she quoted Susan in her story, contrasting her claim to some kind of mystical knowledge of the man who got lost with the ordinary facts she could not come up with. Was there a distinction between the knowledge of love and the statistical approach that was the mark of the bureaucrat? It was the kind of question that always made Amanda feel like an outsider.

Even if it was true that people who live together don't know obvious things about one another, there was no doubt that Susan was a bottomless well of confusion as to what actually had happened on the day Frederick turned up missing.

"He had an appointment with Doctor Carey at one?"

"That's right."

"He knew that and you knew that?"

"We both knew, of course."

"What did you do that morning?"

"Worked in the yard."

"Could you show me what you mean by that?"

The area behind the house was like a mysterious garden in the children's books that had formed so important a part of Amanda's education. She had sought in fantasy the real world of other children and had never doubted that such gardens as this one of Susan's existed. The central path was lined with Japanese red maples, the outer edges were framed with a trimmed hedge of forsythia, but now peonies and irises added contrast to the rich green of the close-clipped lawn. At the end of the path a white trellis wore dozens of roses of a red so rich it verged on black.

"Carnadine," Susan offered.

"They're lovely."

"Roses are easy, if you keep the aphids off."

"What on earth is an aphid?" Amanda was sorry she had asked. It had seemed a Tolkien creature by its name, anything but a pest; it might have been some fanciful negation of Freud.

Far from diminishing Amanda's sense of the garden as a mysterious place, talk of bugs and blights and other enemies of the gardener suggested that even so lovely a place as this could suddenly turn into a menace. The hedge at the back of the yard was thick as a wall and looked carnivorous, as if it could gobble up a man in a minute.

Susan had been pruning her roses on the fateful morning of Frederick's disappearance, but she had done a dozen other things as well. In the corner of the yard was a rock garden from which a small fountain flowed, sending tricklets of water down the rocks into the large, white basin below.

"The same water is used over and over," Susan explained.

"Are those fish?"

Amanda sat on a wrought-iron bench, painted white, and huddled over the pond, watching the colorful fish dart to and fro in the blue, shallow water.

"He must have loved it out here."

"Fred? He hated it. He compared it to putting costumes on animals. Let nature be, that was his motto. Meaning he didn't have a green thumb and resented those who do."

"You certainly have a green thumb."

"Up to my elbow, I think."

The garden sufficiently diverted Amanda that she was willing to accept Susan's claim that on that day she had become so absorbed in her garden that she had not kept an eye on Fred. "Not that he liked to be fussed over. It's always a mistake to treat old people as if they were kids."

"I wish you'd say more on that topic," Amanda suggested, switching on her microcassette recorder.

"I don't have a theory or anything like that. But I made up my mind early on that I wasn't going to baby Fred. Give an old man like that an opening and he will turn you into his slave. Always trying to gain your pity or stir up your guilt. Why are you walking around, spry as can be, while he's confined to a wheelchair? You've got to lay down the law, let them know who's boss. Make them live in the present or they bore you to tears with stories about the good old days."

Amanda shut off her machine halfway through this. There wasn't much she could use, except to give the reader a taste of what poor Frederick had to put up with.

Sometime during that morning, Fred had taken his crutches and left the house.

"Did he do that often?"

"He never did that."

"Like not ever before?"

Susan thought a bit. "As good as never."

"How often did he use the crutches?"

She glanced toward the yard. "I can still see him on that path, propped up on them."

"Just as a guess, how far do you think he could get on crutches?"

She shrugged. "Who's to say?"

"As far as the nearest bus stop?"

"He must have."

"Did the bus driver identify him?"

"Oh, you'll have to ask the police that."

"Lieutenant Morley? What do you think of him?"

"I had all but lost hope before I talked with him."

Amanda said nothing of course, but it didn't really surprise her that Susan thought Morley was just fine. They were two of a kind, if you asked her. For both of them, Frederick was a job: for Susan, someone she had to look after and more or less did; for Morley, one more missing person who could stay that way for all he would do about it.

"Just how do you go about finding a missing person, Lieutenant?" Amanda had asked him.

"You want a fast answer or the whole bit?"

Amanda felt like Lady Macbeth after the "Unsex me here" speech when she talked with Lieutenant Morley. She expected men to notice she was a woman so she could resent their inability to treat her as an equal, and by and large her expectations were realized. A man might go on and on as if he were talking to just another intelligent human being and suddenly he would put an inadvertent hand on her leg and the illusion was gone. She had become adept at discerning the modes of concealment, the various pretenses that she was just one of the guys; these were only more subtle ways of making an approach. With Morley she felt neuter and she didn't like it. A little sexual response from him might even be redeeming, proving he had some human interests, anyway. Of course it was always possible that he had a happy marriage and had no inclination to notice other women. Ha. If she believed that she would get out of journalism. In her experience everyone was flawed. Maybe she just wasn't Morley's type. It was not an explanation she welcomed.

"I want the whole bit." She lifted her chin and looked him in the eye, but she might have been pledging allegiance to the flag for all the rise it got out of him.

"Basically, when you're missing someone you ask the other departments around the state and country to help you and vice versa."

"Does that make sense?"

"The chances are a missing person has left the jurisdiction that reports him missing."

"Him?" She decided to play the feminist card to break through the crust of his indifference. She had his attention for sure.

"Aren't we talking about Frederick Nebens?"

"I thought we were speaking gender-free."

"Most people reported missing have gender."

"That's my point. You should have inclusive language."

"Good point. I'll remember that."

She knew he was being sarcastic, but nothing in his voice or expression betrayed it. She knew it because he had to be. A man his age, socialized as he must have been, would think the effort at gender-free language was an assault on his masculinity. Amanda had taken courses in gender studies and understood these things. Come to think of it, Morley was older than most others on active duty.

"How long do policemen remain active?"

"Policemen?"

"Police."

"How do you mean, active?"

Would his pitch come now? He looked her straight in the eye and it took an effort for her not to blink. "As police."

"You get to retire after twenty years."

"When did you start?"

"A long time ago."

"You mean you could retire?"

"That's right."

"Why haven't you?"

"I'd feel like a missing person."

"I'm beginning to see what you mean."

What he had done about Frederick Nebens was to send information on him along with a photograph that looked twenty years out of date to police departments around the nation.

"You don't mention the crutches."

"They've been found."

"Really! Where?"

"In St. Anthony of Padua church. They were left at the altar dedicated to the saint."

"You are making this up."

He lifted his left hand and joined thumb and little finger. "Scout's honor."

2

LORCH SAT in a corner of the motel unit, a can of Mello
Yello in the hand that hung over one side of the chair, a
leg over the other side, mouth open as he watched television.
He couldn't figure out what the story was and he had been
watching this one for a week, ever since they set up shop in
this hot-sheet place, about to make the score of their lives,
if Casey could be believed. Casey had been in the shower
for forty-five minutes, going for the record, the sonofabitch.
The television got on Casey's nerves so he countered with
the goddam shower. That's how Lorch had it figured. They
hadn't talked to one another for two days.

Lorch cut the sound, got his feet on the floor, crushed
the soda can. He felt like just yelling his head off. Would
anyone care? Casey wouldn't be able to hear him with that
shower pounding out water like Minnehaha Falls. They
might just as well be back in Stillwater, Minnesota, locked

up like this. Except for the TV and shower. Casey's story
had sounded better back there, doing time together, the kind
of inside dope only cons knew. Lorch had listened. It didn't
make a hell of a lot of sense, waiting to get out of prison,
planning something that would put them right back in again.

"Wrong," Casey said. "You think they'd call this theft?"

"I was thinking of possession of a substance."

"It's out of our hands before we touch it."

"How?"

"We line up a buyer before we make our move."

In Chicago, south Chicago, Casey knew where to go because a black guy had given him a contact.

"Black?"

"We call him that because he's my friend."

"He in on this?"

Casey adjusted his pants, tugging at his waist, getting his
belt buckle positioned. This meant he was about to lie. "It's
just a favor."

"Him to us or us to him?"

"Jesus, you're a suspicious sonofabitch."

"From now on. I was before, I wouldn't be here."

Casey leaned forward. "Okay. He didn't tell me. I listened
to him talk, me in the upper bunk, him below, talking to
the man next door. On and on, what big shots they'd both
been. Rains—that's our man—knew all about Chicago."

"How you know it wasn't all bullshit?"

"He was too consistent. This went on for years."

"Things change fast on the outside."

"Look, you don't want in, say so."

Why had he wanted in? He didn't belong in the can, he
didn't belong with clowns like Casey, he shouldn't be wasting
away his life watching daytime television in a roachy motel,

waiting for the big score. He was an almost graduate of De La Salle High School, educated by the brothers, he knew what life is all about. He never missed a day saying his prayers, asking God to forgive him, make him the good thief. At least he wasn't a hypocrite. Yeah, then why did he think he was so much better than Casey?

He came to think Casey was really on to something, that there was a fast score possible here and he knew damned well Casey would double-cross him first chance he got. Lorch intended to get his chance before that. With what they stood to make delivering that one load of hay to south Chicago, Lorch felt he would be ready to try the straight life again.

The bathroom door opened and a soapy cloud of steam drifted into the room. Casey came out, wrapped in a towel, groping on the bedside table for his glasses.

"You gonna pucker up like an old man, Casey."

"That's so my butt can kiss your lips."

"You clean enough to go to work yet?"

Casey got on his black bikini shorts and sat on the bed to pull on his skintight jeans. Cowboy boots, leather jacket, he should have known Casey would be the type. Lorch drove the Ford, he had always been a driver. And he had insisted on the Ford. Casey of course had wanted a Cherokee or a BMW.

"Lorch, what the hell. We ain't done nothing, nobody's looking for us, why not a car we can enjoy?"

"We take a BMW they'll be looking for us real good."

So he selected a Ford from a mall in Rochester, Minnesota, picking up extra plates at the same time. They switched to another Ford in LaCrosse, left it in a toll-road plaza and hoofed it down to the trucker's saloon where they found a pickup. They were due for another switch.

"Why not leave a trail of colored beads?" Casey asked.

They left the pickup in a parking lot across from Trailways in Chicago and took the Amtrak up to Wisconsin.

"Viskey with a beer on the side," Casey said when they were sitting in a booth in the Oasis Bar of the motel.

"Mello Yello," Lorch told Flora, the two-hundred-pound waitress whose tee shirt asked the question "Would I lie?"

"Flora, tell him that stuff will burn away his gut."

"If you tell me why you say viskey."

"Greta Garbo."

Her mean little eyes disappeared in a frown. "Sorry I asked."

"She was a movie star."

"She?" Flora lowered her mouth and raised her plucked brows.

Casey said, "You been away from ladies as long as we have, you'd understand." He tired to pinch her, but couldn't get a grip. She didn't move, just looked at his hand as if it were beneath contempt.

They ordered hamburgers too, with everything, which included number 30 oil. There was a puddle of it in the platter when they were done, and they needed extra napkins to wipe it off their hands.

"Cut out making remarks about where we've been."

"She'll think I meant the Navy."

"There are women in the Navy."

"Wouldn't you like to go to sea on her."

"She'd float.'

"Yeah." Casey looked dreamily at the waitress. Flora had fifty pounds and a foot and a half on him. So far all he'd done was talk tail. Lorch had shaken him awake in Chicago and told him Gladys was ready for him now, but Casey just mumbled and rolled over. Gladys shrugged and made as if to go, but Lorch had her stay. There were three and a half years he was making up for and he liked the way Gladys moaned.

"What were you doing to that woman?" Casey asked the next day. "She howled like she was hurt."

"Moans of pleasure, man. Moans of pleasure."

"Reminded me of the stockyards."

"She reminded me of Greta Garbo."

"Bullshit."

The pawnshop on State Street was the first of three stops. They had agreed that Lorch would stay outside, and he trailed along when the big dude put Casey in the Deville and drove him to the pool hall. That was an hour's wait and Lorch was beginning to think of maybe getting the hell out of there. If he was keeping an eye on Casey, someone could be keeping an eye on him. And then the little guy with gold glasses, fuzzy gray hair and three-piece suit showed up.

"He was the man," Casey told him later just after telling the bartender, "Viskey, with a beer on the side."

"He's our buyer?"

Casey nodded. "He wouldn't say he'd been involved before, but he said he'd take what we bring him."

"Price?"

"Ten thousand a bale."

"How much is that?"

"One delivery."

Lorch eased up his grip on the Mello Yello. Crushing a can when it was still full of soda was a messy business. Casey sat there grinning at him as if he'd just brought off the Brinks Robbery. Ten grand! That wasn't enough to buy a legit car, so why was he smiling? Because he was dumb, that's why. You tell Casey he could make ten grand in half a year at a job that wouldn't put him back in Stillwater or Joliet and he would brush it aside. Chickenfeed. But he was willing to risk his freedom for a lousy ten grand.

"The score of our lives," Lorch said. "I am quoting."

"Say we deliver one a week for . . ." He tipped back his head to figure, one month, four months, half a year. Sure. Just a couple of businessmen. Except there were people in Chicago who would like the goods without having to pay out even a lousy ten grand.

"What about the farmer?"

"What about him?"

"He's going to want something."

Casey grinned knowingly. "And he'll get it."

"Once maybe you can screw him, but not regular."

Casey was getting impatient with all these details. The thing to do was to cut out now. The big score was not big at all, but it was big enough to put them back in the cage. Like an idiot, Lorch had been thinking of hundreds of thousands, a real bundle, something worth taking the risk for. The smart thing would be to take off. No need for any big goodbyes, just go. But first he wanted to switch cars.

"I'll come with you," Casey said.

"What's the point? Drink your viskey."

But Casey shook his head and tossed off the drink. "Look, we're partners, right? Fifty-fifty all the way."

That bothered Lorch. Had Casey picked up the vibes that he wanted to take off?

"I been thinking, Lorch. Why not show up with ten or fifteen bales and make it an all-or-nothing deal?"

"You think the farmer's got that much?"

3

AMANDA POURED the bag of Trailblend into a saucer and pushed it toward Susan. "Try it."

Susan took a pinch and tasted it and was almost disappointed that she liked it.

"It's all natural," Amanda said. "You shouldn't drink coffee, you know."

"Oh, I'm all right so long as I don't drink it after supper."

"I'm not talking about it keeping you awake. Did Frederick drink coffee?"

"Did Fred drink coffee? He should have had a catheter installed he drank so much coffee."

"What do you mean?"

"He peed a lot."

"But what's a catheter?"

"You don't want to know."

On the contrary, Amanda was dying to know. It seemed one more bit of lore that others had and she did not.

"Did he have trouble? Going?"

"His trouble was not going. He called it 'Doing the Incontinental.' "

"You helped him with his bath?"

"The man was a baby."

When they babysat, other girls had a chance to look over little boys and see what they were like, but Amanda had to resort to medical encyclopedias and high school sex texts in which the male organ hung limp as Lake Michigan. In museums she had tried not to stare at what her mother's third husband had called pudenda.

"That of which one ought to be ashamed. Interesting, isn't it?" Number Three was a drunk and a college professor, classics. "One might take it as a pagan recognition of Original Sin."

"Original Sin?"

"As in Milton, my girl."

Number Three always made her feel dumber than she was. But she wasn't dumb, only uneducated. It was two years later that she realized he had meant John Milton.

"Has Frederick telephoned?"

Susan sputtered into her coffee cup.

"It is highly likely that he will," Amanda went on. "Weird people get a kick out of calling those who have a loved one missing and pretending to be him or her. Morley should have warned you."

"I can't believe anyone would be so cruel."

"It *is* disgusting. Has Morley told you anything?"

"Only that there isn't anything to tell me."

"How about your car?"

Susan just shook her head.

"I should tell you that I think the two are connected. You must have been followed to the mall, no one knew you were there, you say you almost never go there."

"I ran into Will Tonsor there."

"And who is Will Tonsor?"

Why did Susan try to laugh while talking? To Amanda, Tonsor sounded like Number Two, a tease, and she could believe that Frederick had considered him a pain in the neck. "Only he didn't say neck," added Susan.

"Did they quarrel often?"

"It wasn't quarreling."

Didn't Susan realize that teasing was worse than quarreling? She had described Frederick as a tease, but that isn't the picture Amanda had formed of the missing man. Sometimes now when she meditated, saying her mantra over and over, she felt that she was in living contact with Frederick, that he knew of her concern for him and took comfort from it. She made up for Susan and Morley. That night, in the lotus position, immobile, mind afloat, free of herself, she asked Frederick what he thought of Will Tonsor. Almost immediately a cramp developed in her leg, and she was crying aloud before she got it untwisted and straightened out. As she kneaded the muscle and the pain faded, she smiled. Frederick certainly answered questions in unambiguous terms.

Will Tonsor, when Amanda met him, even looked like Number Two, tall, smiling over the heads of everybody else, enormously pleased with himself. Number Two had been a counter agent with United Airlines who had been seduced by her mother. He had never flown in his life but had passed on his discount to nieces and nephews.

"How do you get along with your children?" Amanda asked Will Tonsor.

"We had no children."

"What did your wife do?"

"Do?"

"What work? What job did she have?"

"If I couldn't afford to keep a wife I wouldn't have taken a wife."

"She just stayed home all day?"

"My dear young lady, Sylvia was honored by every major organization in this city for her volunteer work. Stay home indeed. I wish she had stayed home more often."

"Has she passed away?"

"In a manner of speaking. She left me after four years of marriage."

It's funny she hadn't left sooner, living with Will Tonsor. It infuriated Amanda to find that Tonsor was into health foods and jogging and ecology and all the right things. Maybe he thought it would bring back caves and he could drag Amy Rordam around by her hair. Susan had told Amanda of Tonsor's infatuation with Amy.

"Tell me about Frederick Nebens," she asked Will Tonsor.

"A cypher. A barnacle on the ship of society. A nonentity. Poor Susan was reduced to being the man's keeper, but it was like looking after an aging pet. The man willed himself into old age long before his time and expected her to pay the penalty."

"That seems harsh."

"Because he's lost? Best thing that could have happened to him. Maybe he'll find himself."

"Have you any idea where he might have gone?"

"I'm surprised he hasn't washed ashore by now. He was a candidate for a jump in the river for years."

Tonsor spoke with strange intensity, doing a little shuffle in his gym shoes.

"You must have been close."

"To Fred? Only by accident. I liked Harry, his son, and of course Susan, his wife. Harry had no idea what he was doing to that woman when he married her."

Amanda found it easier to see Fred Nebens as the subject of her story, even though he was dead. The living, breathing Will Tonsor and little birdlike Amy Rordam fell within the scope of her journalistic interest, old people in America, but there was something intractable about them. She had never known Frederick Nebens, of course. Her image of him, the man who was taking shape as she got ready to write, had been constructed out of dozens of bits and pieces, remarks and the memories of others, particularly Susan. Will Tonsor was a hostile witness.

"Maybe he was a little jealous of Fred," Susan said.

"Because he had you to look after him?"

"No! I meant Amy. Will has a crush on her but she was attracted to Fred."

"Susan, these people are old! What do you mean, attracted?"

"Woman–man."

Susan might have been suggesting that it was beyond Amanda's comprehension. Well, this time it was. Amanda found it preposterous that a man Will Tonsor's age should be mooning after an old woman like Amy. Amy was a girlish little thing, coquettish even. Honestly, there were moments when Amanda felt that she had woken up on the wrong planet. She simply did not understand the natives.

Or she understood them too well. She herself was trying to lead Paul Morley into temptation, just to prove that he was an untrustworthy man, and she found herself miffed by the attention he paid Susan.

"Susan has certainly kept her looks," she suggested to Paul Morley.

He nodded. She mentioned what Susan had told her about Amy and Will and Fred, and he just shrugged.

"I guess it's in the genes," she said.

"I prefer you in skirts."

So she had gotten a rise out of him after all.

4

"WHAT'S THAT smell?"

"Grass?"

Casey sniffed again, then let out a sound of pain. "What do you mean grass?"

Having cleared the area where they picked up the car, Lorch turned on the lights. He liked the car, but it sure did smell.

"Ever smell new-mown hay? Neither did I. When I was a kid, I was a caddy and behind the caddy shack was where they dumped the grass after mowing. Same smell."

"There's a sack back there."

"Check it out."

"Bullshit. Let's get another car. That smell is making me sick."

Obviously he had made the picking up of cars seem too easy for Casey. Try one out, you don't like it, take it back for another. Sure. And run into the guy who owns the car you're returning. Maybe they'd picked a lemon, but they were going to stick with it for now. Casey was rolling down the passenger window. Lorch pushed the button that lowered the back window.

"Better?"

"Compared to what?"

Casey was a complainer, no doubt of that, except when they were doing something he had decided on; then everything was perfect. They had been here three days and hadn't even talked to the farmer, hadn't even seen the farm. This seemed as good a time as any to have a look.

"Look, Lorch, pull over and let me get rid of that sack, okay? I'm serious. It's making me sick."

"Smoke a cigarette."

"C'mon."

"Wait'll we get out in the country."

"Country? What are you talking about?"

"I want to see a man about a farm."

"Hey, wait, not now. That's my call, man, and it's not time."

"You want to tell me what the hell we're waiting for?"

"Precautions."

"Tell me about it."

For the first time since Chicago Casey made sense. He wasn't as dumb as he seemed, after all.

"This business, Lorch, always keep your ass covered, know what I mean? We been to Chicago, a couple businessmen, promising to make a delivery. Lots of dudes would like to take that burden off our hands. Far as I can see, nobody's on us, but I want to be sure."

"As long as we're out here, you want to pitch that bag?"

Casey shrugged. Lorch pulled over and cut the lights and motor. Turning off the engine seemed to turn on the crickets. The night hummed with them. Lorch opened his door and it seemed the sound must carry for miles. Casey was reluctant to get out.

"Would you do it?"

Lorch slammed his door and went around to the back and let down the back flap. He grabbed the bag and pulled it toward him, not expecting it to be so heavy. He untied the neck and reached in. Grass, just grass. And then his hand met another hand.

"God almighty!" he jumped away from the car.

"Whatsamatter?"

"Come here?"

"What is it?" Casey's door pushed open and he groped his way along the side of the station wagon.

"Feel in the bag."

"Tell me about it."

"There's a body in there."

Casey hesitated, but then he began to pat the outsides of the bag as if frisking it. He felt a foot, then a face.

"Geez. What do you think?"

"I think we picked the wrong car."

"We?"

"We could just leave it here."

"Wait. Let's think about it. This is crazy. A station wagon parked in a mall lot with a body stuffed in a plastic bag. What do you make of that?"

"Take a look at the body."

Casey's revulsion had disappeared. He was caught up in the excitement of the problem. Lorch found a flashlight

in the glove compartment. He also started the motor and
turned on the ceiling light. He turned them off immediately. From far down the road came the hum of an approaching car.

"Get the hell into the car," he yelled to Casey.

"He may turn off."

"Get in!"

Casey pulled up the back flap and got into the passenger
seat, a disgusted look on his face. Lorch got the car rolling
and soon a pickup came over a rise and went past them.
After a minute, Lorch pulled over again and hopped out.

"We going to do that every time we hear a car?"

"That's right. So let's hurry."

Casey stripped the bag open, grass falling out as he did
so, and the clawlike hand Lorch had felt came into view. It
was like a horror movie. Casey held his nose with one hand
and exposed more of the corpse. An old man.

"Cover him up," Lorch said.

"You suppose he crawled in there and died?"

"The top was sealed."

"No shit."

Casey dumped the grass back in and hopped in beside
Lorch, who was rummaging around in the glove compartment. He found the registration. Susan Nebens.

"You know who that is?"

Casey looked at him. "You do?"

"It's the woman who reported her father missing. It was
on the news yesterday, old guy supposedly just disappeared."

"Into a sack." Casey shook his head.

"We can take it back to where we found it. I don't think
she's going to file a complaint."

"You think she left the car there?"

"Who knows? It's possible. What I do know is that we don't want to be cruising around with a hot car and a body besides."

"Her address there?"

It was. Lorch wished Casey were still gagging over the smell. He had the crazy look on his face he'd had when he knocked over the filling station in Wisconsin, just for the fun of it. That kind of fun could spell the end of their vacation from Stillwater. Fooling around with a corpse that was none of their business was the same thing.

"Let's drop the car off at her place."

"What the hell for?"

Casey punched his arm. "Think of it. She's lying about the old man, probably meant to dump him off somewhere and she comes out and her car is gone. I mean, think of what she's thinking."

"You want to drive this car to that address, you're welcome."

"We're partners!"

"To do one definite thing, that we haven't got around to yet. Okay, I think you're right about stalling to see if someone is checking us out, but we're here to do that, not to crap around with a body in a bag."

"But think of her reaction!"

Lorch wished he hadn't told Casey about the missing old man. He wished he didn't have the stupid habit of reading the paper.

"Maybe she didn't leave the car in the mall."

"You mean it was hot before we took it."

We. "Could be."

"Geez." In a minute Casey was telling another story. Someone kills the old guy and steals the car and then when the paper and TV go nuts about it he abandons both in the shopping mall parking lot.

"We would be returning her loved one."

Lorch drove back to the motel and parked the station wagon on the other side of the building, at the edge of the lot, as far from their unit as he could.

"What if it's found here?"

"That's the idea."

"I don't like the idea of the place swarming with cops."

"It's not our car."

They wiped it down before they left it. Casey looked back at it as they crossed the lot. "Poor old sonofabitch."

"I'll buy you a viskey."

"With a beer on the side?"

And Casey grinned from ear to ear.

5

WHEN HE wasn't telling Amanda Tracy about all the missing persons who stayed missing, Morley was answering calls from Amy Rordam, who seemed to have appointed herself honorary widow in prospect of the missing Fred Nebens.

"What roughly is the percentage of missing persons found?" Amanda asked, notebook at the ready.

"It's surprising how many turn out not to have been missing."

"Meaning what?"

"They escaped, ran away, alone or with someone else, they were gone but they weren't missing. Step One is to figure out whether you're dealing with one of those or with someone genuinely lost."

"When do you plan to get to Step One?"

Sweet kid. He gave her a stack of files to look through

and went into his office to take a call. It was Amy Rordam. Felipe Alou and his brother Jesus!

"I just remembered something I thought might be significant."

"Shoot."

"I beg your pardon."

"What is it that you've remembered, Miss Rordam?"

"Higgins Lake."

"Higgins Lake?"

"He vacationed there as a boy. He spoke of it with real nostalgia, tears in his eyes. He made it sound like heaven."

"You think he went to heaven?"

"Lieutenant Morley, I don't think that's a bit funny. A man is lost, a man seventy-five years old. God only knows what has happened to him, and you joke."

"I'll put through a call to the police in whose jurisdiction Higgins Lake falls."

"Is that all?"

Did she expect him to go to Michigan himself and prowl the Lower Peninsula because an old man had once talked wistfully of time spent at a lake as a boy? How could he be out giving tickets to tax-paying motorists if he did that?

"I'll let you know if they find him."

"What else are you doing?"

"I've got hundreds of police forces scouring the nation. His picture has been faxed everywhere. Cops on the beat are looking for him."

"Here too?"

"Here too."

"Do you know what I keep thinking of, Lieutenant? Those pictures of missing children you see on milk cartons. Are any of them ever found?"

"Have you ever seen those pictures of kids on milk cartons?" he asked Amanda Tracy when he went back to her.

"They haunt me," she said, and he believed her.

"How many do you think are ever found?"

"What happens to them?"

"There's a real story for you. You think they're all just lost? They've been kidnapped by pornographers and white slavers. Most will be introduced to drugs and when they're hooked they become hookers. The lucky ones end up in Near Eastern harems."

"This is known?"

"Known but not provable. Not to satisfy a court. Besides, the lawyers that show up to defend anyone suspected of such things, well, they're the best money can buy."

Amanda looked pensive, as if the corruption of this vale of tears came as news to her. Did she think everyone was trying to be a good citizen, anxious about the rights of others, altruistic, a crusader like herself? Crusading was just another way of bashing the system. Not that it wasn't bashable. What isn't?

"Police work has made you cynical."

"After you've been in your job a few years you'll be no girl scout either."

"Did you ever think of writing?"

"To whom?"

"I never know when you're serious."

"Let's have lunch. I'm serious."

"As long as it's on the paper. This is business."

Why not? They went to Chez Angelo where the special of the day was spaghetti alla carbonara, and she thought he was being funny when he tucked the checked napkin into his collar. The vino della casa was a local red. "Made in his basement."

"It's good."

She smiled and looked like Dracula's sister. This stuff would dye his denture but what the hell, it was good, if you like sweet wine. "Tell me about yourself."

"This is my lunch, on the paper, I get to ask the questions."

"That's all you do, only you never listen to the answers."

"I not only listen, I record them, in writing and on tape."

"But you don't understand."

"Explain it to me."

"The chances are that as we sit here enjoying our pasta, Fred Nebens has been dead for days. We're not looking for a living man but for a corpse."

"You can't possibly know that."

"It's been what, three days? A guy that feeble wouldn't have gotten a few blocks from home, let alone out of town. If he's in town, walking around, somebody is going to notice him. That hasn't happened."

"So he left town."

"So he's lying dead some place."

"What a dreadful thing to say."

"Just remember I said it. Your story on Fred Nebens is what went on before he disappeared," said Morley.

"You're telling me how to be a journalist?"

"Just because you've been giving me lessons on how to be a cop? Not on your life."

"How old are you?"

"About as old as you think."

"I'm thirty-two."

"I never would have believed it."

She smiled prettily.

"I mean, all that experience."

The smile faded. He put his hand on her arm. "I have a daughter your age."

"Oh God."

"What's wrong?"

"That is so old. You feel like a father to me."

The fact is, he didn't. He felt the way he did about the Widow Brady. Come to think of it, he had felt pretty horny around Susan Nebens too. Maybe hot flashes would be next.

"Are you a widow?"

She made a face.

"What was your father like?"

"I don't know."

"You don't remember or what?"

"He died in Vietnam. I was just a kid. All I have is pictures."

She looked away, pulling her lower lip between her teeth as tears leaked from her eyes.

"I was there too."

She turned to him, looking at him suspiciously through wet eyes. She wouldn't be kidded about this.

"Early on, before the real shit started. I was there when Diem was killed."

Every time he made out an expense sheet, he thought of the murdered statesman. Here's to you. Per diem. That whole thing had stunk. Now it could be told. Kennedy authorized or looked the other way, and the man was assassinated. And then came Kennedy's turn. The war had started out badly and ended worse.

"What year was that?"

"1963."

"My father was killed in '65."

"Spumoni?"

"Sure."

"How about your mother?"

"Not while I'm eating. She played musical husbands until her luck ran out."

"I'm beginning to understand your naive outlook on life."

"Naive! I'm what is known as a tough broad."

"Then why are you trying to make a fairy tale out of an old man's end?"

"We don't know that anything has happened to him."

"And do we really know the moon isn't made of green cheese, underneath the rubble, that is. I mean, let's keep an open mind."

She drank the last of her wine and smacked her lips approvingly.

"When are you going to retire?"

"Did I say I was going to retire?"

"Everyone retires."

"It used to be called vulcanizing. Recapping. New tires out of old. Funny about words. Take entrance. The way in. And what I do to you."

"Ho ho."

"I have a friend in Florida, retired. We visit them now and again. I don't want that."

"What's your wife think?"

"You should interview her. Spouse of cop in charge of incompetent investigation. A nice touch."

"What does she think of Frederick?"

"I never asked her."

"Don't you talk about it?"

Amanda probably had a wacky notion of what marriage is like too. What was it like? Not a question he'd care to be asked.

"Are you married?"

"No!"

"It's not indictable."

But he wasn't in the mood to defend the institution of marriage. He and Ginny got along, more or less, which seemed about par. If Amanda wanted to think her mother was a fair sample of the married woman, let her. What was her opinion of an aging husband who, like her father, had fought in Vietnam but, unlike him, had lived to tell of it?

Back at the office they learned that Susan's station wagon had been found.

"Fred was in the back. Stuffed in a trash bag."

"No!"

He did not say "I told you so."

PART FIVE

1

THE CAR was parked in the Palm Beach Motel on Route 33 north of town, and Morley got there before they moved it. How the hell had it ended up here? Park and his assistants were wearing masks as they examined the contents of the plastic bag. Morley used a handkerchief. He wanted a look at the old guy. Death hadn't improved him any. There were blades of grass sticking to his face and clothes. A hand reached out as if to be shaken.

"How long he been dead?"

"How long he been missing?"

"Three days."

Park dipped his head. "About that long. I'll give you a more precise answer later."

"How'd he die?"

"His rib cage is crushed. Run over? I don't know."

"Check the car."

Park nodded. The car would be trucked in and examined thoroughly. Park removed his mask and lit a cigarette without apology. He spent his day among the dead and was unaffected by health warnings. "Tidy, bagging him up like that."

"After running over him?"

Park frowned. "Maybe after he was put in the bag. We'll check on that. In the bag. Do you know the phrase?"

"I know the condition."

All the bullshit about wanting to live long, yet people hated the aged. Why? Morley didn't know why, but he had felt it himself, an irrational resentment at the sight of old women, their bodies sagging and bloated, shuffling along, but still capable of a girlish giggle. And the sunken-faced old men with their wary eyes. Why do we hate them? A reminder of the fate that awaits us all, maybe, if we're lucky, if that's luck.

The meat wagon came for Fred and the truck came for the car and Morley crossed the lot to the Palm Beach. No curiosity had been shown by the motel clients about what was going on in the parking lot, but then those who came to the Palm Beach didn't see much more than the insides of their rooms. The place featured X-rated movies, magic-finger mattresses and a quick turnover. The man behind the desk was short, but what was visible of him was huge. It turned out that he was already standing. A black tee shirt, bald head, side hair hanging over his ears, gold necklace. Morley showed his ID, but Muscles didn't change his expression.

"Let's see your book."

He reached under the counter and got it.

"We found a stolen car and body in your parking lot."

"Yeah?"

Morley turned the page to three days before. No Fred Nebens had registered. You never knew. Porn movie houses are filled with old geezers you'd think were beyond all that. Maybe Fred didn't want to die without having seen a really dirty movie.

"Who are these guys in 12?"

Muscles turned the book around and looked. "What it says. Casey and Lorch."

"They been here five days."

Muscles looked at him expressionlessly.

"How often do you change the movie?"

"Ask the boss."

"I thought you were the boss."

The muscles in his jaw tightened. Was he flattered or insulted?

Morley left it at that, but when he got downtown he ran a check on Casey and Lorch. Bingo. What were they doing this far from home and only weeks after being released? Murdering old men didn't figure in the M.O. of either one of them, but you never knew when an artist would decide to expand his standard repertoire. Morley assigned Wayne to keep an eye on them.

"What am I looking for?" Wayne patterned himself after television cops, which should have made him useless on stakeouts. Baggy sweatshirt, long hair, untied Nikes, Indian jewelry—what else could he be but an undercover cop?

"I don't know. Check in at the Palm Beach, drink at the Oasis bar, see what you see with those two."

"Give me a clue."

"A hot car with a body in back was found in the parking lot today."

"And they're still there?"

"If they haven't left while you're sitting here asking questions."

Amanda's suggestion, if it was even that, was William Tonsor, though she couldn't say why a man that age would run over another man that age.

"He sweet on Amy Rordam too?" asked Morley.

"Too?"

"Amy acts like the man's widow."

"How has Susan taken the news?"

"Want to find out?"

He might just as well invite her to go with him since he would have to reconstruct it for her afterward if she wasn't there. Besides, he liked her company. She reminded him of his daughter, as he mustn't say to Amanda, that being the ultimate ruse for getting a young lady into bed. On the other hand, she missed her father a lot. Maybe his inclination ran to more than widows. This would give him a chance to compare her with the Widow Nebens. He told himself to shut up and keep his mind on his job. The night before he had slid in beside Ginny and scared her half to death.

"What do you want?"

"An orgy."

"Paul, don't be silly."

He got a hand between her arm and ribcage and squeezed her breast. "Does that feel silly?"

"Your hand is cold."

"Warm heart."

"Oh my God."

But he could almost hear her smile in the dark. She was wearing a nightgown and didn't want to take it off.

They might have been trying to do it in a tent. All in all, it was like winning at wrestling, but that's the way Ginny had always been. You want it, go for it. If she ever just flopped for him, he might have been unable to rise to the occasion.

"That it?"

"Couldn't you tell?"

"If memory serves."

He patted her ass, and she gave him a good hit on the thigh, bringing on a near charley horse. Once she read aloud the beginning of a story of Tolstoy's, about happy and unhappy families. He thought the Russian had it all wrong. The unhappy families Paul met on the job were as predictable as sin. More or less happy couples, like Ginny and himself, worked it out in all kinds of different ways. They were happy, weren't they? Sort of. Of course there was always the lingering thought you were missing out on something. Think of Vic and Martha down there in Okefenokee country and be content.

Amanda drove her own car, of course; she couldn't be dependent on the police.

"Would *you* ride with me?" she asked.

"Just name the place, pardner."

He let her beat him there, knowing she would wait to let him be the one who gave Susan Nebens the bad news. But that grim task had already been performed by Park, who'd asked Susan to come down for an identification. He would have to have a word with Park. Goddammit, this was his case.

"It was your father-in-law?"

She sat at the kitchen table, staring from Morley to Amanda and back. "Yes."

"I'm sorry. Maybe I should have prepared you for this."

"He's been dead all this time," Amanda said, as if stating a grievance.

Susan nodded. Her lack of emotion stirred Amanda's sympathy, and she put her arm around the older woman's shoulders.

"You got coffee on?" Morley asked.

"Make some," Amanda suggested.

But Susan stirred. "I'll do it. Does Amy know?"

"Was there something between Frederick and Amy?"

"Air," Susan said, and burst into tears. "That's what Fred used to say." She was sobbing helplessly now. Paul Morley preferred this to the way she had heard the news. Surely she must have considered the possibility that something had happened to her father-in-law.

"We'll release your car to you as soon as it's been gone over."

"What do you mean?" She turned from the coffeemaker.

"Didn't Park tell you about the crushed rib cage?"

"He said he had been run over by a car." She looked at Amanda and horror registered on her face.

"We'll want to know if it was your car that did it."

"Can they tell that?"

"We'll see."

"Why would anyone run over an old man? Was it an accident, do you suppose?"

Amanda looked at Morley and then looked away. "Do you think we should let Amy know?"

It turned into a goddam tea party, although coffee was served, and Morley asked himself what he was doing wasting away the afternoon like this. He called home and told Ginny he'd be working late.

"I'm going out anyway."

"Oh."

"I told you."

"Remind me."

"Phyllis and I are going to the mall."

Some movie. He remembered now, remembered the unexpressed irritation that Ginny was going anywhere with Phyllis. Phyllis was a divorcée, a childhood friend, trouble.

"Have fun."

"You sound as if you wished I wouldn't."

If this wasn't a phone conversation it could easily escalate into a quarrel. Ginny knew what he thought of Phyllis. She asked why he wouldn't be home.

"Old Nebens has been found dead. I'm here with the daughter-in-law, Harry Nebens's widow."

"How's she taking it?"

"The news? All right."

"How old was he?"

"Older than I am."

"That's hard to believe."

"You were wonderful last night."

"Shut up. And don't wake me up when you come in tonight."

"That's what I was going to tell you."

But she had hung up.

Back to work. What did he have? The missing person he'd been on was no longer missing. Old Fred Nebens shoved into a plastic bag half full of cut grass had turned up in his daughter-in-law's stolen station wagon parked behind the Palm Beach Motel. Staying in the Palm Beach were two ex-cons only recently returned to civilian life. If they had been there and gone it would be more promising. It didn't make a lot of sense that they would do Fred and then stick around, let alone park the body behind the motel. His task had altered from finding Fred to finding how he had died. Lorch and Casey weren't a lead, but what else did he have? And Wayne had nothing else to do.

part of an hour. He was drinking seven-and-sevens, at least, which made him more company than Lorch with his Mello Yello. Mello Yello is so full of caffeine it keeps truckers awake, but Lorch swilled the stuff as if it were sleeping medicine. Never trust a man who doesn't drink. Who'd told him that? What Casey didn't like about Lorch was the guy seemed to think he was doing him a favor, coming in on a score like this, all set up and thought out, foolproof.

Lorch was in a corner playing the games. He was good at them. Casey never went near them. Some day he'd go off and practice, then come back and beat the shit out of Lorch, that would show him, but he wasn't going to go up against him without practice. The guy at the end of the bar was determined not to look this way. Casey wished he'd asked the bartender about the guy before saying that about Flora.

On the giant-screen television there was a tennis match from Rome that no one was watching, but it was better than the soap operas Lorch watched. Casey had thought he was watching women's tennis until the long-haired player scratched his balls and he realized it was a man. Looked like the guy at the end of the bar. Lots of turnover in the Palm Beach, wham, bam, thank you, ma'am. Lorch'd had some in Chicago, but they were both cherry since coming here. Casey hadn't had a woman since getting out. It wasn't that he was scared, except maybe of disease. All you read about now was the diseases you could get doing it. He'd had the clap as a kid and that was as bad as he wanted it, and he was tough enough to be left alone by the queers at Stillwater. Bitchy bastards, they all but ran the place, but now with AIDS they threw their weight around less. Probably all of them due to die of it anyway. Good riddance, as far as Casey was concerned. Don't fool around with Mother Nature. The Catholics had it right. You got that thing for a reason and if you don't acknowledge it, watch out. Look what was happening all around. People thought they could screw everything in sight and things would be the same. That was why he was so damned careful, but he wasn't going to explain it to Lorch.

Lorch reclaimed his stool, and the guy from the end of the bar walked by on the way to the john.

"Who's winning?" Casey asked him, hunching his shoulder at the television.

"Who's playing? I haven't been giving it much attention."

"Sit down here when you come back." Casey patted the stool beside him.

"Who's that?" Lorch asked when he was gone.

"That's what I want to find out."

"What the hell do you care?"

"I don't. Just curious."

His name was Wayne and he had taken a unit in the motel, thought he might look around for work. Anything manual, he didn't care. He liked being outside.

"Where you from?"

"Memphis."

"You don't sound like it."

"It paid not to where I been."

Casey looked at Lorch, wishing he'd made a bet. To Wayne he said, "I'm thinking of making a bid on this lamp."

"I don't think they'd miss it if you took it."

Maybe he would, when they left. Back in the unit, Lorch was still mad about Wayne.

"The car's gone."

"I noticed."

"There were cops around all day. Funny they didn't check out the motel."

"Because someone abandoned a car in the lot? Nobody did that's going to be staying in the motel."

"I hope you're right."

"Look, we haven't done anything. We're clean."

"We're a long way from home."

"Relax."

He relaxed with the local paper, which was full of the story about finding the old man's body, though it didn't give the Palm Beach a free mention, which showed they attached no importance to where it was found. Even so, Casey talked to Earl at the desk.

"What's all this about a body in a car?"

"It's all over with. It's in the paper."

"I seen that. Cops talk to you?"

Earl said no. When he shook his head, his eyes didn't move. Casey practiced it back in the unit and couldn't do it. Not looking at himself anyway. He couldn't tell if Earl was lying either. He didn't say anything to Lorch. The smart sonofabitch never even thought of asking Earl. It dawned on Casey that it had been dumb to leave the car here at the Palm Beach and that had been Lorch's decision.

Two days after the body and station wagon were found, they drove out to the farm in a newly acquired car. If Wayne was watching them for the Chicago connection they should get themselves another boy. Whenever Casey looked into the bar, Wayne was there, sipping on seven and sevens. The guy must be an alcoholic. He ought to switch to Mello Yello. He might never get any sleep, but his head would be straight.

The farm was a hundred and forty acres in the bottom land along the river south of town, the fields full of eight-foot-high stalks of corn. The grass was planted between the rows, put in after having been started in the plastic-covered greenhouses. Barth and his wife picked the marijuana by hand and cured it in the barn. He had been Peace Corps and picked up the habit in Laos, but he was Mister Straight as far as the neighbors went, or so Casey had learned from his black buddy Rains in Stillwater.

"When did he last deal with him?" Lorch wanted to know.

"A big black guy down here dealing with whitie the farmer? Come on."

"He just heard about it?"

"Look, we check it out. If it's true, we hijack the whole crop."

"We better check to see how many German shepherds he's got."

"We'll check everything." Why the hell did Lorch have to mention dogs? If there was one thing Casey was truly scared of it was an angry dog. As a kid he had had to pass barking dogs on his way to school no matter which way he went. Every time he thought he'd got past them one would bark at his heels, and he had to walk very slowly because if he ran they ran too and really nipped at him then. That was when he stopped believing in God. Every night he would pray that those dogs would leave him alone, and the next day there they were. That farmer had dogs, they were dead and no mistake. He had gotten the gun in Chicago as part of the deal.

"Where's that thing been, you know that?"

"It's clean."

"You have it on the word of a man you know would kill you for twenty bucks' worth of grass."

"You sound like someone itching to get out of this deal."

"I just don't want it fouled up."

"That's your worry, huh?"

"Let's take a look at the fields."

"Now?"

The sun stood high in the sky; across the fields the expanse of the river glittered in sunlight. Casey had the feeling he was hearing noises from miles away. He could see that he was. On a barge a man the size of a bug lifted and dropped his hand and what seemed a minute later the sound came. He went on, hammering away, the sound track out of sync with his action. Weird. Was someone watching them from far away, or closer?

"You wait here." And Lorch went down the gully and scrambled up the other side and disappeared into the corn. Casey was after him, still holding the gun, not wanting to be left on the road alone. The stalks crackled as he entered the field, dividing before his hand, and his boots sank into the soft, dry ground, which was almost sandy. How could anything grow in that?

"You see anything?" Lorch was out of sight but spoke right next to him.

Not between the rows where he was he didn't. "It'd be farther off the road."

He followed the sound of Lorch going deeper into the field. The stalks snapped back into your face if you didn't hold them away after making a step, and Casey got mad, using both hands in a swimming motion.

"I wish I had a machete," he yelled, but Lorch did not answer. Casey stopped. Everything grew still. The slightest breeze, but it made a little rattling sound as it passed through the dry corn. Smelled good too, Casey noticed, the breeze stirring up the smells of the field. It was like being imprisoned in a cereal box. Where the hell was Lorch? He was just going to stay where he was, while he still had a good idea where the road was. He put the gun away, tempted to use it on a crow that suddenly lifted out of the corn a few feet away, scaring the bejesus out of him. Damned farmer feeding the animal world too, birds, raccoons, everybody waiting around for the crop to come in, no wonder the man decided to diversify and add to his income. Who the hell would suspect another crop concealed by this one?

"Casey?" Lorch was speaking in a normal voice and it was hard to tell how close he was.

"Yo."

"Say something and give me a bearing."

"You lost?"

"Not unless you are. Keep talking."

"You telling me you don't know the way out of here?"

And then there he was, his face pushing through the stalks. He grabbed Casey's arm and spun him around, moving him toward the road.

"Hey, what the hell?"

At the edge of the field, Lorch gave him a push and he tripped, falling ass over tea kettle into the gully. He rolled over but before he could get up, Lorch had his foot on his chest.

"All this cornfield's got in it is corn, buddy, now what do you think of that?"

What Casey was thinking of was getting out the gun, but he didn't want to make the move while Lorch had that size twelve on his chest. Calm, he felt very calm, as if everything had been moving to this. He took in what Lorch said in a minute, right away he knew it was true. He could argue the point, how could they tell on one pass of a field, but Casey had the flashing realization that all along he had been conned by Rains, all that talk of grass just waiting to be taken and sold for a fancy price to Rains's friends in Chicago. Only in the can could you believe that kind of luck awaited you on the outside.

"Nothing there?"

"Corn."

"Shit."

"That all you got to say?"

"Take your foot off my chest."

"Did you know there was nothing here all along?"

"No!"

"You're sure not acting surprised."

"No." Casey took Lorch's shoe and moved it off him. He sat and made a few dusting motions at his clothes, then stood. "No, I ain't surprised and do you know why? This is my whole cotton-picking life summed up here. Work my ass off for something only to find it wasn't there in the first place."

Lorch's expression softened, as if Casey was describing his lot as well. Casey turned as if to climb out of the gully, then wheeled with the gun in his hand.

"All right, you sonofabitch, stand right there."

Lorch laughed. He just stood there in the gully he was going to die in and laughed as if he meant it. Casey waited for him to finish. He did not want to shoot a laughing man. He was holding the gun in both hands, out in front of him, trained on Lorch. Lorch's laugh settled down into a fixed smile. He made a couple of passes at Casey, fake ones, teasing him, as if he were a bull. Okay, bastard. Casey pulled the trigger.

Nothing.

He pulled it again and again and the only sound was that of the hammer against the lock. Lorch was on him then, tearing the gun from his hands and knocking him on the side of the head with it. Casey fell to the left and Lorch caught him in the gut with his free hand, and Casey felt he was being lifted off the ground by the strength of that one blow. The air was out of him and Lorch let him fall gasping to the ground. Trying to breathe, Casey watched Lorch clamber up out of the ditch. Casey was on his knees, still unable to take in air, when the motor started. He crawled out of the gully but never did see the car, only a great cloud of dust being kicked up on the dirt road as Lorch disappeared.

PART SIX

1

AMANDA HAD told Susan that in cases like this creepy people might phone, claiming to be Fred, and want to talk to her about the next world, that sort of thing, but there had been nothing at all before this eerie call.

Susan, they found the old man in the garbage where you put him.

The echo of that voice in her mind sent shivers through her. Not that Susan needed any outside help to feel that she had desecrated Fred and that Harry somehow knew about it and hated her for it.

There were times, early in the morning, when she first came awake, that she was sure none of this had happened. She could not possibly have run over Fred, then hidden him in the garbage and pretended he was lost. That was bad enough, but to put him in a trash bag and drive him around town seemed worse than a bad dream, made only more incredible when the car and Fred were stolen. All her stupidity had been due to a desire to escape criticism and questioning, but now she knew she should tell Paul Morley everything. And she would have, if it hadn't been for Amanda.

"Of course people blame you," the reporter said. "If someone has to be blamed, it's the person who's devoted her life to caring for the missing person. I'll bet even *you* feel guilty."

"Oh, I do."

"It's perfectly natural. And, after all, who is perfectly innocent? I mean, through and through. Amy says Frederick could be very difficult at times."

"Amy Rordam doesn't know a thing about it."

"Was Frederick aware of Amy's, well, interest in him?"

"It's pretty obvious, isn't it?"

"Isn't it odd that a woman can go through a long life unmarried and suddenly, at twilight, desperately pursue a man?"

Was that natural too? Amanda pretended to have such a vast fund of knowledge of the human heart. Susan was not sure why she had permitted this confident young woman to intrude into her life, ask questions about herself, comment on her friends, speak of Fred as if he belonged to her. She liked Amanda or at least respected her, but she could hardly think of her as a friend. Sometimes, with Morley, she had the truly silly feeling that Amanda was a rival. The lieutenant brought back bittersweet memories of Harry, but Paul Morley had a wife already.

"Are you married, Amanda?" Susan asked, sure that she wasn't.

"Would it affect your estimate of me if I were?"

"Estimate?"

"As a working woman."

As far as Susan could see, Amanda was paid to do what

anyone would love to do, snoop into other people's business, enjoy the luxury of not taking sides, at least not openly. If Amanda didn't have the excuse of being a reporter, she'd be as bad as Amy.

"You're single?"

"Let's just say it's irrelevant."

What a peculiar young woman she was. The only reason Susan asked was the way Amanda played up to Paul Morley. Did she consider it irrelevant that he was married? But the sense of censure would not come. Susan found it all too easy herself to have thoughts about Paul Morley, thoughts that would have been a cause of shame at any time, but now, in the wake of Fred's death, were doubly awful. It helped a little, only a little, to remind herself that Paul Morley had known Harry. They were practically boyhood friends. But she had the pleasant feeling that Paul was not thinking of Harry when he looked at her. Such silliness!

"I suppose I should check out with you the things Amy has told me." Amanda was dialing her cup around its saucer with her index finger.

"What things?"

"Well, about Will Tonsor."

Susan got up from the table, to get the coffee pot, but also to get away from Amanda's relentless questioning.

"Susan," Amanda went on, "let's face it. If it was only Frederick, we could treat it as a horrible accident. Somehow he managed to get downtown, he imagined he was cured when he visited the church, he was struck down and killed when he went outside again. Okay. That would have been one thing. But now your car is taken and, lo and behold, when it is found Frederick's body is found in it, stuffed into the trash bag of lawn clippings you had in there."

How simply linked the events were. All that was needed, as Amanda patiently explained, was a person to link them.

"Me?"

"Susan, be serious. Now I want you to think of Will Tonsor as you probably have never thought of him before."

"Oh now, you can't possibly . . ."

Amanda, with closed eyes, shook her head and patted Susan's hand. "Listen first. I know this will seem fantastic. But Amy and I already walked through it, and it is possible."

Susan listened, if only because her sense of being at last driven into a corner lifted while Amanda spoke. She and Amy had actually imagined that Will Tonsor had run over Fred as he came out of the church.

"God knows what resentment welled up in him when he saw the object of his teasing walking along as spryly as anyone else. He might have directed his car at Fred only half voluntarily. That is why he stopped and helped Frederick into his car, not realizing how seriously he was injured. Quite soon he had a dead body on his hands."

The Will Tonsor Amanda imagined was indeed a totally different person from the man Susan had known. The fact was that he and Fred had liked one another, liked having one another as enemies, so to speak. Besides, what Amanda was suggesting was as incredible as the truth. Stealing her car, stuffing Fred in the trash bag, abandoning the car in a motel parking lot—it was all preposterous. But was it any more so than what actually had happened? Wouldn't others react to the true story as she reacted to the story Amanda and Amy had made up about Will Tonsor?

Amanda wasn't sure that Will's actions were meant to harm Susan. "We'll get the facts when he decides to tell the tale, and I wouldn't be at all surprised to learn that he really didn't have a consistent purpose in mind. Stealing the car might have been an afterthought. When did you last see him?"

"At the mall."

"At the mall! When?"

"The night the car was stolen."

Even as she said it, she realized Amanda would take it to be proof positive that her fantastic tale was true. "Will had opportunity, he had motive."

"What motive?"

"To get rid of the body. How did he react when you saw him at the mall?"

A literal description would have presented a slightly manic figure, boyishly active, chattering, smiling, in short, the usual Will Tonsor, the Will Tonsor who had made Fred grind his teeth in rage. "What's the sonofabitch always bouncing around for? He's got ants in his pants or maybe his shorts are too tight. More likely the problem is inside. The man's compost mentis."

"You mean non compos mentis."

"No, I mean shit head."

She told Amanda that Will had acted perfectly normally that night at the mall.

"Have you told Paul Morley about seeing him there?"

"No."

"Why not?"

Why would she tell Lieutenant Morley about a meeting that had decided her against putting poor Fred's body in a dumpster? If the car hadn't been stolen, Will would have been the unwitting obstacle to the desecration of Fred's body. She would have driven home and she would have telephoned Morley and the whole nightmare would have been over, no matter what shame or punishment she faced. She had acted in a completely indefensible way for the basest of reasons, and she deserved whatever was coming to her.

But someone had stolen the car. Someone had discovered the body in the bag. Somebody had found her name on the registration card. And today that somebody had telephoned.

"Susan Nebens?"

Whoever it was, it was a stranger, and she said what Amanda had told her to say. "I can take a message."

"I'll bet you can, Susan. Well, they found the old guy in the garbage bag where you put him."

She hung up. It was not fear she felt but fury. If what she had done became known she wanted it to be by her own initiative, not as the result of another's accusation. The phone began to ring again. Susan sat looking at it until it stopped ringing.

She felt that she had conjured up the caller as an explanation of what had happened to Fred. What would Paul Morley think if he knew she was letting him chase after the supposed murderer of Fred when the whole thing was an accident? A preposterous series of events. Too preposterous to tell anyone now, and far too preposterous for anyone to believe. She couldn't tell Paul and she couldn't tell Amanda—it would make a mockery of their efforts. Amy?

"Will there be a viewing of the body?" Amy had asked.

"No."

Amy mastered her disappointment. "Have you seen him?"

"I had to."

"You should have had Will Tonsor identify him."

But Susan had had to see Fred. It was so tempting to tell herself that she could not have done what she had done, that was not the kind of woman she was, certainly not the kind of daughter-in-law. She had devoted herself to Fred.

She expected no congratulations for that, it was her duty to Harry, if nothing else. And people knew that she had been good to Fred. She imagined telling Amanda the truth, pretending it was a terrible dream she'd had, but she couldn't even do that.

"I think there should be a viewing of the body," Amy said.

"Fred wouldn't want that."

"It's not for Fred, Susan. It's for others."

Amy seemed intent on playing the role of Fred's widow. If she had any sense she would pay attention to Will Tonsor.

2

WILL TONSOR had buried most of his friends, and at his age it was no longer possible to work up a big emotional reaction at the news that somebody else had crossed the great divide. A moment of surprise soon passed, and then he subconsciously added another name to the roll of those who, unlike Will Tonsor, hadn't hung in there, kept breathing in and breathing out, refusing to give up and grow old. There wasn't even the element of surprise in the case of Fred Nebens. The old guy had been missing for days, and what more or less surprised Will was the realization that he wouldn't see the old fart again. Fred would be missed, if only because he had always been good for a pointless argument. And Will had to admit there was some distinction in the way Fred had gone.

Tied up in a plastic bag of grass clippings? Amy seemed to begrudge him the information when he cornered her in the mystery section of the library.

"Jesus," Will said, and Amy crossed herself. "You Catholic?"

Amy gave him a look. "Of course not. But I have a great devotion to Saint Anthony of Padua."

"Who's he?"

"Look it up," Amy suggested, gesturing toward the reference section. But Will was thinking of Fred tied up in the plastic bag.

"Then it couldn't be suicide."

"Suicide! Of course it wasn't suicide. There is every reason to think that death was brought on when he was struck by a car."

"He'll be missed."

Amy tolerated the cliché. She seemed to be waiting for him to say more, and Will wondered if this was his moment. Grief, profound emotion, her defenses trembling. He reached out for Amy's hand.

"What are you doing?"

"The ranks are thinning, Amy," he said mournfully. "Survivors ought to stick together."

She was moved by the remark, no doubt about that. Tears began to run from the corners of her eyes. Will tried again to take her hand, but she snatched it away and ran from the library. At the desk, Brenda Bowles looked at the disappearing Amy and turned to Will.

"What's wrong with her?"

Will looked sheepish. "Several people told me she has a crush on me, but I had no idea . . ."

"Isn't she a little old for you?"

How pink and plump and succulent Brenda looked, peering at him over the lenses of her glasses. Will had the unaccustomed feeling that any and every woman was now ready to drop like ripe fruit into his lap. He patted Brenda on her plush little hand.

"Checking anything out?" she asked.

"Just the staff."

"Promises, promises." Her bowed little smile dimpled the corners of her mouth.

"I'm thinking of starting on an extended reading program."

"Maybe I can be of help."

"I'm counting on it."

And he pushed through the stile and through the revolving doors. There was a jauntiness in his step as he went out to his car. He was sure Brenda was watching him go. When it rains it pours.

"How's the love life?" Matt Hilliard asked, stopping at the putting green where Will was pushing orange golf balls through the fallen leaves.

"My cup runneth over."

Hilliard nodded as if he had been vindicated, and Will crouched over the ball. He had thought of getting one of those putters with the chest-high handles, so he could putt standing upright. But it was easier to concentrate when stooped over. He lined up the putt, drew back the club, brought it cleanly forward. The ball scooted across the surface, crackling through leaves, into the hole. Hilliard clapped but Will said nothing. It wasn't the hole he'd been aiming at.

3

LORCH TOLD himself he should have changed cars and just kept going, maybe to Florida, somewhere out of the Rust Belt to sun and easy living. The Palm Beach had nothing but a name in common with what Lorch thought of when he thought of Florida. Funny how he always sided with southerners against his fellow northerners when those arguments arose. "If Dixie's so damned nice why you doing time in Stillwater?" "Just being in the North is doing time, Stillwater or no Stillwater." Half kidding, half serious, on and on, but Lorch liked the image of the gallant loser. And it was true that southern whites got along better with blacks. Blacks from the South hated the North as much as anyone else. Casey was a racist, but you should have heard him go on about slavery, as if the South had invented it.

Casey was a pain in the ass and Lorch knew he was a damned fool for having gotten mixed up with him. It was hard to believe he had actually listened to the little guy talk big score as if he had ever known one in his life. He knew a man who knew a man, and all they had to do was do what any idiot could do and they were rich. But there wasn't any call for a middleman because there was nothing to deliver.

After taking off, leaving Casey on the road behind waving his arms like crazy, Lorch had stopped and gone into another part of the field, just to make sure. He came up empty there too. Boxcars full of grain are sampled by running a long tube in at random, and what is brought out stands for all of it. Lorch made two samplings of the field and there was nothing growing there but corn. When he went back to the car, Casey was in the passenger seat, staring straight ahead, working his jaw.

"That sonofabitch," he said when Lorch got behind the wheel.

"Who you calling a sonofabitch?"

"Rains, that's who. The only score here is the one he made conning me." He turned to Lorch. "Listen. We never came here, understand? We never believed the man in Chicago."

"And you never tried to shoot me."

"Aw, the gun wasn't loaded."

"Because I unloaded it. You don't get no credit at all."

"You think I don't know when a gun's loaded or not?"

"I don't think you know which end of it you put in your mouth."

Casey stared straight ahead again, working his jaw, and Lorch got them out of there and back to the motel, parking the car a block away, not far from where he had picked it up, a convenience to the owner. Wayne was in the bar when they went in there. Casey pounded on the bar. "Viskey," he shouted. "Gimme a viskey."

"With a beer chaser," Wayne said, and Casey joined him.

Lorch left them, stopped at a bottle store where he bought a twelve-pack of Mello Yello and then went back to the unit with the newspapers—the Chicago *Sun-Times*, the Milwaukee *Journal*, the local rag.

Old Fred, the body they'd gotten with the station wagon, had been taken to the crematorium after a ceremony at the funeral home conducted by a Unitarian minister. Had the old guy been a Unitarian? There was no mention of him being a member of the church. In Stillwater, Lorch had been what the chaplain called a connoisseur of religions, going to whatever service was on, comparing ceremonies, sermons, how farfetched the promises made. There were two classes of padres, those who thought they were doing prisoners a big favor and those who seemed to envy prisoners. "I was in prison and you visited me" was the favorite text of the first, "I have suffered shipwreck, I have been imprisoned" the favorite of the second. They thought what was good enough for Paul was good enough for anyone and the boys in Stillwater ought to appreciate the honor. There were variations within these two groups. The Catholic chaplain was in a class by himself. He came in and did the Mass, reading from a book, not making anything up, and when he said a few words about the readings he gave the impression that that is what they meant, not what he had to say about them. His name was Finn.

"As in fish, as in five, as in Helsinki. I've heard them all so don't bother. It's an Irish name. How long you been here?"

Lorch told him.

"First time?"

He told him of Faribault and the other place, in Kansas. Finn toted it up and pointed out that he had done all that time for a grand total of one thousand seven hundred dollars.

"I'd give you that much if it'll keep you from coming back."

"I'm not coming back."

They looked at each other, neither one of them believing that. Lorch asked Finn if he believed in fate.

"Only when things are going badly."

"You think we act freely?"

"I think we act freely because we do. It's not an opinion."

There it was again, Finn the retailer of truth, not its manufacturer. Some day Lorch intended to look into all that again. He was glad Finn couldn't see him holed up in this moldy unit in the goddam Palm Beach Motel, buddied up with Casey who was a retired Catholic, fated to lose, the kiss of death. And Lorch didn't like the look of Wayne either. Maybe Casey would buddy up with Wayne and Lorch would be free of him that way.

It said in the paper that Fred was survived by his daughter-in-law, Susan Nebens. That was the name on the registration of the station wagon. What in the hell was she doing driving around with that old man in a plastic trash bag? Casey was bothered by the same question.

"Wayne knows who she is," Casey said.

"He from around here?"

"I guess."

"Why's he staying in the goddam Palm Beach if he lives in town?"

"You want to know, ask him, will you? You wanna hear the idea I've got?"

"Oh my God."

Casey smiled and nodded. "Go ahead. I deserve it. We got made asses of and no mistake. But I've thought of a way to balance that off before we leave town."

Casey had on his monkey grin and he adjusted his pants, getting the buckle right.

"Okay, don't ask me, I'll tell you. We drove all the way down here and came up empty and I'm sorry. But knowledge is power, as the man said, and we know something. We know something about a lady's car and a bag in it full of old man. We saw her park that thing, no one put that bag in there while we waited, so she knew it was there. Now why's she driving around with a dead man in her car?"

"He's too heavy to carry?"

Casey laughed, too hard. "Go ahead, I deserve it."

"What's your idea?"

"We put the arm on her. Wayne says she's got money."

"You talked with Wayne about this?"

"Wayne? You crazy." Casey got off the bed again and glared at Lorch. "You've used up what I owe you, all right? What kind of a dumb bunny you figure I am? You're my buddy, or supposed to be."

"I'm good for target practice."

"That didn't happen, okay? It was a big mistake, but God was looking out for both of us."

"God?"

"This idea is so good I truly believe it came from Him."

"He wants you to go out and shake down widows and orphans?"

"What orphan?"

"She's the only survivor."

"Listen, it's a cinch. Anything in that paper telling what we know she did?"

It was the kind of thing that might work. Simple. *We know something you don't want known. Ten thousand in cash by tomorrow night or we tell everything we know.* She doesn't have to know they sure as hell weren't going to go to the police station and swear out a complaint against Susan Nebens. Lorch liked it. But everything depended on the first contact. If she showed fear, they went ahead. If she laughed it off, that was it, drop it. Casey agreed.

"You want to call her or should I?"

"It's your idea."

He pretended to read the paper while Casey made the call. The first time, she hung up, but Casey kept dialing the number until she listened. From this end of it the conversation seemed to be going the way they hoped. Casey asked for ten thousand.

"And we want that in used bills, no numbers recorded. Anything funny and you join Fred, understand?"

He put the phone down gently and turned to Lorch.

"I think we got her."

"She's got ten grand?"

"We'll know tomorrow."

Tomorrow before five she was to put a plastic trash bag containing the money in the dumpster in the mall parking lot. No police, come alone.

"I thought the trash bag was a nice touch," Casey said.

"Very nice." And Lorch meant it. Maybe the little monkey would turn their trip into a paying proposition after all.

4

WAYNE CALLED Morley to say that the two jokers at the Palm Beach Motel were asking about Susan Nebens.

"Well, one of them of is, anyway. The one called Casey."

"What's he ask?"

"Her age, is her neighborhood a good one, does she have money?"

"And you told him what?"

"I just answered the questions."

He hadn't counted on Wayne being that dumb, but there didn't seem to be much point in chewing him out now.

"That completes your assignment, Wayne. Come on in."

"You're kidding. They're getting ready for something. Last night they drove out into the country and began running around in a cornfield."

"That make any sense to you?"

"No, but it sure as hell makes me curious. They came

back mad as hell at one another. Then Casey started to ask about Mrs. Nebens."

"Good. That's fine. That's all I wanted to know."

Wayne argued the point for five minutes, another sign he wasn't the man for the job. He should have wondered why his boss wanted him out of the Palm Beach and that should have suggested to him that maybe being such a mine of information about Susan Nebens would make him vulnerable. Morley could've told Wayne about the number of stolen cars that had been showing up within a mile radius of the Palm Beach.

"You're the boss," Wayne said sullenly.

"At least for now."

He couldn't blame Wayne for thinking those two were up to something. They hadn't come all this way from where they belonged just for the ride or to enjoy the appointments of the Palm Beach Motel. Whatever it was, it wasn't worth jeopardizing Wayne for.

"There's something you can do, Wayne, and you'll appreciate the importance of it."

"Yeah?"

"Do a stakeout on Susan Nebens. Just to make sure nothing happens to her."

"That's what I was going to suggest!"

"Great minds."

His own great mind was devoted to establishing a connection between Fred Nebens and Lorch and Casey. Had those two been sent here to pay a very old debt, kill Fred Nebens before nature did the job? Those punks were too young to have had anything to do with Fred so they would have been doing the job for someone else, but who? Fred had run a downtown barbershop for years, one notorious for its football pools in the fall, a form of gambling which, while technically illegal, was a harmless amateur enterprise. But had Fred's been an amateur enterprise? Asking around among cops older than himself, Morley could find no one who would completely rule out something funny at Fred's barbershop. The mob had come and gone in this city for years, and a barbershop is a nice locale for running the rackets, particularly with that innocent football pool as cover.

"Did Fred talk much of his days as a barber?"

Susan rolled her eyes. "He had six chairs at the peak, but he was down to one, his own, when he closed up shop."

"Five assistants?"

The barber's union had lists and records but only one of the barbers who had worked for Fred was still active, Mr. Leonard in the mall. Mr. Leonard had a meaty nose, a mane of curly black hair that reached to his shoulders and a very small waist that looked corseted.

"Fred? I heard. How terrible."

"You worked a chair in his shop?"

Mr. Leonard laid a hand on his arm and looked over his shoulder. "Let's go in back."

Back was a room with shelves full of the pomades and hair colorings and other potent concoctions that gave Mr. Leonard's customers the illusion of beauty and/or youth. "Sure, I cut for Fred." He spoke normally now, cupping the cigarette he'd lit. "The fairy act is for the ladies. They love it. When I look down their blouses they figure it's jealousy rather than lust. And if I pat their ass, it's just between us girls. I was really sorry to hear about Fred."

"Pretty awful way to go."

"Running over an old guy like that, geez." He shook his head and dragged on his cigarette.

"Maybe it was on purpose."

Mr. Leonard's luxuriant brows rose. "Who the hell would want to kill Fred?"

"That's what we're trying to find out. There are a couple of hoods in town that seem linked with the accident. Was there ever any mob connection at Fred's shop?"

"Mob! Don't ask me. I never heard, never noticed." He stopped and dragged on his cigarette. "I sound like those three monkeys. I don't think so."

"There could have been?"

"That sounds like I know something and I don't. I really don't."

"Remember the football pool?"

"Remember? Look, I won once and Fred wouldn't let me collect. Said I shouldn't have bought a chance, it would give the pool a bad name. I guess I saw his point."

All the department records were on computer and Fred's name came up three times. Once when his shop was robbed, after hours; once when a man had a heart attack while being shaved; the third time when his body was found in his daughter-in-law's station wagon.

"Funny they would steal your station wagon, put Fred in that, and then leave them to be found together," Morley said to Susan.

"I've given up trying to understand what happened."

"Your car was stolen from the mall last Friday night?"

She sighed. "Yes."

"Why'd you have that trash bag in the car?"

"I've got a confession to make." She leaned forward, looking him directly in the eye. A moment passed, then another. She sat back. "I was going to throw it in the dumpster there in the parking lot."

"Why?"

"There were days before my trash pickup. Do you know what cut grass smells like after a while?"

"There's still a bagful in the garage."

"It was a test run."

"You still got Fred's things? Mementos, albums, that kind of thing?"

"In the attic."

"Can I see them?"

The attic was low and warm and close, and Susan stayed with him to show him Fred's things. She crouched to pull out a wooden crate, her skirt rode over her knees and Morley got a glimpse of the promised land. Memories of the Widow Brady were intense. How long had it been since Harry died? Susan was still a young woman and she'd been a lot younger then. What a future Harry's death had left her with, a widow and the caretaker of Harry's old man. It was like throwing herself on the funeral pyre of her husband. Had she just checked out, sex-wise, gone into escrow in that department? For someone else that might seem easy enough, but of course that was due to a lack of imagination.

A wisp of hair fell over her face and she puffed at it to get it out of her eye, but it returned to where it had been and that became an accompaniment of her showing Morley Fred's trophies and mementos—a little puff, the hair blown away, then falling back where it was, a moment and then another puff. It was cute and it was unconscious. Susan's figure was still good, firm, enough of everything, not too much.

"This is Bernie Bierman's signature," she said, showing him a team picture of the Minnesota Golden Gophers. "Whoever he was."

Morley let it go. Real women were supposed to be dumb about sports. He took the picture from her and their hands touched. She didn't pull away, and he held her hand as he studied the picture. How warm it was in his. He was sitting on the floor and she was crouched beside him. Without looking at her, he pulled her toward him. She lost her balance and fell into his arms. He held her tightly and listened to the blood roar in his ears. The silence of the attic was a sensuous envelope pressing them more tightly together.

From below came the sound of the telephone ringing.

"Don't answer it."

She pushed free of him. Her face was flushed. "I lost my balance," she said, throwing her voice toward the end of the attic.

"So did I."

Their eyes met. The phone rang again. She scrambled to her feet and went downstairs. Listening to her voice, indistinct below, he felt at once elated and foolish. What a stupid thing to do. Yet he sat there in the hope that she would return and it would be as it had been during the dizzying moment he held her in his arms.

"Paul?"

He turned to see Susan's head appear from the stairwell.

"That was Amy. She says there's a long-haired man prowling around, watching this house. She's right. I can see him."

"Don't worry. He's one of my men."

"One of your men?"

"To watch over you."

Her face grew flushed again and then disappeared.

"I'll be downstairs," she said. "Look as long as you like."

PART SEVEN

1

AMANDA TRACY was finally impressed by Paul Morley. Assigning an undercover man to watch over Susan was one of a number of sensible things he had recently done.

"I didn't know Belting had undercover men."

"That's the point of them."

She peered at him. "I won't even ask what that means."

"A man doesn't brag about being good under the covers."

"Honestly, I'll have to warn Susan about you."

"I'm surprised she hasn't told you."

"Told me what?"

"Of her futile efforts to seduce me. She lured me into the attic and tried to work her evil will on me, but I slipped away."

She stuck her tongue out at him and he returned the favor, and there was something devilishly suggestive in the way he wiggled his brows. Amanda had the awful thought that she was becoming like her mother, after every man around. But the only man around was Paul Morley.

"How old are you anyway?"

"That's what Susan keeps asking me."

Was he trying to make her jealous? Jealous! Of what, for heaven's sake? Maybe he *had* tried to take advantage of a woman who was going through an intensely stressful experience. Amanda would ask Susan about that. It might even qualify as sexual harassment. Why did the thought make her so angry?

"Why don't you just arrest the two convicts at the Palm Beach Motel?"

"I'm beginning to regret I told you about them. You're not to write a word about those two without clearing it with me, understand?"

"Censorship?"

"In the interest of the safety of citizens, you're damn right. You wouldn't want to do anything to jeopardize Susan Nebens."

So he did fear those two thugs might do something to harm Susan. Amanda decided to take a look for herself. She got into what she thought were clothes that would enable her to blend in at the Palm Beach, but every head turned when she came into the Oasis Bar and the fat proprietress, Flora, waddled over to her.

"What can I do for you, dearie," she said in unfriendly tones.

"I thought I'd have a drink."

"This isn't your kind of place. Take a look at my clientele."

A little peek into purgatory or worse was Amanda's reaction. She beat a retreat. A good idea, that visit to the Palm Beach, reasonably well executed, but impossible to bring off.

She decided to add her own protection to that of the under-cover man.

Fortunately, she and Susan got along well and the older woman would not find it odd that she spent a lot of time with her. After all, Amanda would immortalize her father-in-law in print.

"His end was not typical, of course, but it adds to the story."

"What is the story?"

Amanda put it together for Susan. The calls she was getting? If they were from the men at the Palm Beach, Casey and Lorch, and if they had stolen Susan's station wagon and were responsible for Fred's death . . .

"Why would they harm Fred?"

"Do you know what a hit man is? Fred was involved in gambling, in his barbershop."

"You're not going to write all that in the paper!"

"Of course not."

Not unless it made more sense than it did now, anyway. Amanda found herself thinking of Casey and Lorch. She could not help regarding them as members of the oppressed underclass, the object of a relentless police investigation that would very likely put them back in prison where they had already spent most of their adult lives. There had to be a better way.

"We could arrange for the two of them to be made Eagle Scouts," Paul Morley said.

"Funny."

"Or they could sue the prison system for incompetence. Doing time was supposed to reform them, and here they are getting into trouble again."

He might joke about it, but he had enough sense to provide protection for Susan.

The undercover man was actually more than one. Sometimes he was a middle-sized person with long hair and outlandish clothes, a little obvious Amanda thought, who sat slouched in a rusty old Pontiac reading *Mad* magazine. That had to be Wayne, and at first he refused to meet her eye. She stood beside the car until he rolled down the window. She was surprised to see that he was at least as old as she was.

"Has Lieutenant Morley told you about me?" Amanda asked in a low voice.

"Who's Lieutenant Morley?"

Amanda got out her press card. He studied it for a moment before putting on glasses.

"And you're Wayne."

He sat up and took notice of her. "Morley send you?"

"I've just come from the Oasis."

"Stay out of there."

"I can take care of myself."

He looked at her over his glasses. Lovely blue eyes. Amanda imagined him as he would look with his hair cut, or at least shampooed. And shaved. He could be a lot better looking than Paul Morley. And it was nice of him to be concerned about her.

"What story did you tell your wife when you were staked out at the Oasis?"

"What wife?"

"I'd better get going," she said, not moving.

"Stick around. I have no secrets left."

"Later."

She meant when it was all over. Maybe. After that she made a point of not noticing Wayne, although she was sure he took notice of her.

Sometimes Susan's protector was a small, wiry man who

wore an oversize black leather jacket and cowboy boots and looked right through her so Amanda didn't wink. He must have been the backup since Wayne was between him and the house. He was also less frequent or at least less visible. Wayne could have taken lessons from him, if the idea was to see without being seen. All in all, Amanda felt safer while visiting Susan than she did in her own apartment.

"Lieutenant Morley here?" she always asked on arriving.

"Why do you ask that? He doesn't live here."

"Did I suggest that? Or did he?"

"Amanda, he's a married man."

"So? All's fair in love and war. And he's obviously attracted to you."

Susan blushed prettily and Amanda admitted she was jealous. She had faced up to this fact only that morning as she brushed her teeth. Her hair was nice, but her teeth were her crowning glory. Large, white, even in a not-quite-wide-enough mouth that gave the impression that she had more than her quota. She flossed, she used an antiplaque mouthwash, she brushed for ten minutes in the morning and another ten at night. She had had one cavity in her life.

"Not counting your mouth," Doctor Orlon, the family dentist, said. While he worked on her she had been fascinated by the hair on his bare arms. He had a way of resting an elbow against her, of holding her face, that seemed unnecessary. Amanda never complained or mentioned it to her mother and later realized that she had been the dentist's unwitting accomplice. Men like him counted on a submissive reaction and of course everything had been ambiguous. Now she knew all about men, most emphatically including married men, and she had been prepared to fend off Paul Morley. It was annoying that he chose to pester Susan rather than herself. She had tried leading him on, first, to protect Susan, who was in a particularly vulnerable state at the moment, and, second, to have the chance of using the various put-downs she'd been rehearsing as she brushed her teeth. More and more she thought of Wayne. She was sure he would act as a man was supposed to and she would be able to put him in his place.

"Amy says there's more than one cop watching the house, but Paul says she's imagining things," Susan said.

"Paul? I'm surprised he admitted there's one."

"Anyway I'm glad."

"Have there been any more phone calls?"

Susan's eyes grew round as she nodded. "Paul said I mustn't talk about it."

"It can be off the record until later."

Susan looked doubtful. "Amanda, I didn't tell him all of it."

"Tell me."

They were knee to knee in the kitchen nook, with cups of coffee on the table before them. Amanda brought her cup to her mouth and looked receptively at Susan.

"They want money. A lot of money."

"Why should you give them money?"

"I lied to them too. I told them the police don't know."

"But why do they think you'd give them money?"

"I don't know!"

Susan seemed almost as surprised by her shouting as Amanda was. It was important to remember the stress the poor woman had been under and the greater stress she was under now.

"How much money?"

"Ten thousand dollars."

A large sum of money, as Susan said, yet somehow it

seemed low. Doubtless they were just preying on a woman in distress. Maybe they thought she was a rich widow. Maybe she was, in a sense.

"What are you going to do?"

"What can I do?"

"Well, you're not going to give a couple of hoodlums ten thousand dollars just because they ask for it. Susan, I am sworn to confidence, as I promised, but you have to tell Paul Morley."

Amanda liked the idea that Susan hadn't told him yet. Of course Amanda had already told her that threatening calls were the kind of senseless thing she was subject to in her present circumstances. Strange little people wished to include themselves in dramas they read of in the paper. They telephoned those involved, whispering obscenities, making threats. What possible basis could anyone have for extorting money from Susan Nebens? It made no sense and if Susan were thinking clearly she would see that. Paul Morley should have warned her of this kind of thing.

"Susan, have you eaten?"

A sheepish look. "I've been doing little else."

"I was hoping you'd offer me lunch."

"There's some Waldorf salad left."

"Oh, I love it."

"So does Paul. With lots of raisins. I made it for him."

"I'll have some anyway."

Susan laughed girlishly as she got up from the table. Amanda wondered why another person's folly's so obviously such. Susan was a woman of some intelligence, she still had her looks, she was finally released from the great burden of looking after her father-in-law, however unfortunate the circumstances of that release might be. She had every right to be considering what interesting things she might next do. Travel, for example. Enroll in a night course. Write her memoirs. Yet here she was permitting a married detective older than she was to flirt with her, and taking seriously a crank call demanding ten thousand dollars.

"There's also roast beef. I could make sandwiches."

Amanda nodded fervently. She didn't ask if the roast had been prepared for Paul Morley too. She made a note to drop by the Morley home and interview his wife, just background for the story she was writing, and it would provide an opportunity, out of sisterly solidarity, to drop a few hints Mrs. Morley might want to follow up on.

The sandwiches were delicious, the Waldorf salad only so-so. "Too many raisins for my taste."

"Is the beef too rare?"

"It's perfect."

"I'm sick of it." Susan began to wrap up the meat.

"You're not going to throw that out?"

"Do you want it?"

Want it? Of course she wanted it. She wanted all kinds of things that were full of cholesterol and bad for her. She was torn between shock at seeing good food thrown out and her highly rational diet.

"Make up some more sandwiches and I'll give them to the lookout man. I'm sure he'd love them." It seemed only right that Susan should provide the occasion for her to talk again with Wayne.

Susan made two sandwiches, wrapped them in waxed paper and put them into a sack. She picked an apple out of a bowl and looked at Amanda. "What do you think?"

"Sure. Do you have a beer to put in as well?"

"He's on duty. He can drink Coke."

"I'll take it out to him."

"Why you?"

"Because you're under protection, that's why. Technically, you don't even have to know he's out there, and it certainly won't help him if you go out and say hello."

"Is he out there now?"

"He's always out there."

"I suppose I should be grateful."

"Tell me more about the phone calls."

"I'm glad you told me calls would be made."

"You think this is a crank call? I suppose you're right." Amanda realized she was disappointed. "Only a nut would expect you to give him money."

"Paul wants me to lead him on."

Amanda nodded. That was one way to find out who it was. But Amanda began to think that the call meant nothing. Ransom made sense only if the caller had something Susan wanted.

She almost forgot the lunch when she left. Susan came to the door and called her back, handing her the bag. Making a face, Amanda took it and started up the street.

Nothing in the first block. She was looking for the old rust bucket with Wayne in it, but then she saw parked in the next block, all but hidden behind another car, the little fellow. He had a partner with him today, probably because Wayne wasn't around. She walked up to the car, holding the bag up before her. The little man's eyes grew large and his mouth fell open.

"Look what I brought."

"Is that it?"

He was out of the car now, and snatched the sack from her.

"Inside," the driver growled.

The little man took Amanda by the arm. "The back seat."

"Look, I've given you that, now I'm going." She was startled by this reaction to the sandwiches. But the man tightened his grip on her arm, painfully, and forced Amanda into the car, the back door having been opened by the driver. A final shove tumbled her onto the back seat in an undignified manner and she completely lost her balance when the car took off. She righted herself, but they turned a corner then and she was thrown back against the door. Surprise gave way to anger. She was willing to cooperate with the police but this was too much.

In the front seat, the little man was tearing open the sack, and the driver kept turning his head toward him as if he expected the car to steer itself.

"Watch where you're driving," she yelped as the world rushed at them.

"Sandwiches!" The little man turned, and his face was twisted with rage. "What the hell you mean bringing us sandwiches?"

He threw one of them at her. She tossed up her hands to block it and Miracle Whip ran down her arms. The driver rescued the other sandwich and began to eat it.

"A ten-thousand-dollar roast beef sandwich," he said, speaking with his mouth full, and Amanda finally understood.

2

BEHIND THE wheel, Lorch began to laugh. He was driving with one hand, holding the goddam sandwich with the other and laughing besides. Casey figured he'd be lucky if Lorch didn't run into a wall. What the hell else could go wrong? In the back, the broad sat in the middle of the seat, her face pale, looking as if she was thinking of jumping out first chance she got.

"What the hell you bring that sack of sandwiches to this car for?"

She wouldn't look at him. A little cry escaped her as Lorch made a wild turn, almost rolling the car. Casey grabbed her wrist and pulled her toward him, leaning over the seat so that their faces were inches apart.

"I asked you a question."

"Your breath reeks."

Lorch snickered and Casey looked furiously at him. "Will you stop the goddam laughing and drive."

"You shoulda had your sandwich, Casey. It's all the pay we're going to get."

Casey feinted a punch at the woman, but it was Lorch he wanted to hit. She curled up in a corner of the back seat and looked at him the way most women did. At least she was crying. He tried to think. If he had the gun with him he'd have shut them both up so he could figure out whether this really did mean the deal was off with Susan Nebens. He got as calm as he could and then turned around to face the broad. She stopped crying as soon as she saw his face; she knew he meant business. Too bad he didn't have the same effect on Lorch. Well, that sonofabitch was going to get his before this was over, that was settled now. Lorch still chortled as he wheeled the car along, slower now, a good citizen.

"Why'd you bring those sandwiches?"

"It was meant as a lunch, for heaven's sake."

"You brought us a lunch?"

"Yes!"

"Why? Don't turn away, goddam it. I want to know why."

"I thought you were taking Wayne's place."

"Wayne."

"There's been a policeman assigned to look out for Mrs. Nebens."

"She thought we were cops," Lorch hooted. "She thought we were cops." He slowed and looked back at her, "Lady, do we look like cops to you?"

"She mentioned Wayne."

Lorch shut up when he figured that out and, by God, if he had laughed again, well, Casey would have taken a lot of time when he got around to doing him. Oh, Lorch was gonna pay. The sandwiches had been a mistake. That was point one. Of course he'd figured Susan Nebens wanted to get ahead of schedule, avoid the mall, get the thing over with, give them the money today. What else was he supposed to think when the broad waltzed up with a paper bag saying I got something for you? She hadn't thought they were who they were, how could she? Lorch was right. She had thought they were cops. Because Wayne was a cop and Wayne was keeping an eye on the place because Wayne would know what they looked like and that meant Susan Nebens had not kept her word. Okay. Laugh, Lorch, you bastard, but all this added up to pluses as far as Casey was concerned. When he started to spell it out for Lorch, Lorch waved him off.

"I get the picture."

"So don't say we came up empty."

He looked over his shoulder, then at Casey. "Okay, we didn't come up empty. We can't go back to the Palm Beach, that's for damned sure."

"I can."

"There's nothing there worth the risk."

"Just one thing."

The gun. He didn't have to say it, Lorch understood. "Casey, forget that thing, it only means trouble."

"You think we aren't already in trouble?"

Finally something he said got through to Lorch. He seemed to sag a bit behind the wheel. What the hell did he think he'd been on, a Sunday-school picnic?

Lorch parked on the street behind the Palm Beach and Casey cut between two buildings, crossed the parking lot and was into their unit without being seen. He loaded the pistol while he was at it. He packed up—why leave anything?—and put the bag out behind the unit. There was one more thing he wanted.

There was no one in the Oasis but the bartender. When

he saw Casey he slapped a glass on the bar and reached for the whiskey.

Hell, why not? "With a beer chaser," Casey said, and the guy lit up like the lamp he had come for. "Unplug that thing, will you?" he said when the shot and beer were in front of him.

The bartender frowned. "I don't know."

"It's all right." He brought out the piece.

The bartender unplugged the lamp and pushed it toward Casey, who tossed off the whiskey, then sipped some beer. "Remember Wayne? The guy who used to sit right over there."

"Yeah."

"He's a cop."

The bartender thought about it. "Naw."

"I'm telling you. Tell Flora. That's my payment for this."

He ran into Flora in the hall and gave her a pat on the ass for old time's sake.

"Hey, where you going with my lamp?"

"The barkeep will explain it."

And he kept on going, picked up his bag and was out the door to the parking lot. He began to run then, excited, scared. It seemed a helluva lot longer going back. When he reached the far side of the street he came to a stop, huffing and puffing and looking wildly up and down.

There was no car and no Lorch and no dame. Casey stood there with his suitcase in one hand, the hula girl lamp cradled in his other arm, and wanted to cry. It was like being ditched when he was a kid.

3

SUSAN TOLD Paul that Amanda had been to the house and left, taking a bag of sandwiches with her. Paul looked at Susan.

"Sandwiches?"

"That roast beef you liked? She thought Wayne might want a sandwich."

"She took him a sandwich?"

"When she left."

"But he just came on duty."

"Maybe she missed him."

Morley went upstairs and looked from the window of the front bedroom and saw one rusty fender of Wayne's car. He hoped Wayne had a better view of the house. Susan offered him a mug of coffee when he came downstairs.

"Today's the day," he said. On his instruction she had told the caller that she would get the money he demanded.

"I haven't heard from him."

"You've got the money?"

"Mr. Wilson sent it this morning." She smiled. "He had the mailman bring it."

"Brilliant."

She looked at him. "Was it your idea?"

"I said it was brilliant. Susan, no matter what happens, you'll get it back."

"I wish the whole thing was over with."

"We just wait now for the call."

"What if they know I've told you?"

"They will assume you talked to the police whether or not you did. But they can't know. Not unless they've been watching the house, and in that case Wayne would have recognized them."

But she continued to look worried. Well, he was a good deal more worried than she was. According to Wayne nothing had been going on, nothing, no suspicious people, certainly not the two from the Palm Beach. Morley wished he could be confident of Wayne. He spent much of his time on stakeout reading magazines and tossing his hair. How could a man stand having long hair like that? But then some men like beards. Twice Morley had begun to grow a beard, but after a few days he'd been glad to shave the stubble from his face and feel clean again. Wearing a beard was like having a dirty face. Wayne objected to having the magazines he read called comic books.

"Aren't they funny?"

"They're witty. Did you ever read *Mad*?"

"Not yet."

"Maybe you wouldn't like it."

"Why so?"

"It's pretty subtle."

"Oh, I don't know. I like you."

Well, it was a lonely job, just sitting there all day, waiting for something to happen and hoping it didn't. The fact that Wayne had talked to those two cons at the Palm Beach bothered Morley more than anything else.

Waiting for the phone call wasn't a barrel of laughs either, despite the company of Susan. She was too nervous to keep her mind on gin rummy.

"I talked with William Tonsor," he said, as much to pass the time as anything, and her reaction surprised him.

"Will you please stop listening to Amy Rordam? It's absolute nonsense that Will Tonsor had anything to do with what happened to Fred. Anyone who knows Will would realize that in a moment."

"Actually, he called me."

"What for?"

"He said he didn't want to bother you, but wanted to know if there was anything he could do to make things easier for you. I thought that was kind of nice."

"What did you tell him?"

"That I'd ask you."

"I can't imagine what it is he thinks he could do."

"Maybe he thinks you're lonesome not having an old man around."

"With you here all the time?"

"Hey."

Her smile was the nicer for being rare. She hadn't had much reason to smile lately and ever since the episode in the attic, the big move that never happened, she seemed a little skittish around him. Who did she have? Will Tonsor and Amy Rordam didn't fill the bill, but it was too bad Susan had no relatives, some close friend her own age, female of course.

"I'm sorry about the other day."

"What do you mean?"

"The attic."

"Nothing happened."

"I said I was sorry."

Before her smile fully formed she turned away.

After a decent interval he said, "Amanda must be a real break from me."

"If she wasn't so full of theories about things she has no experience of." She turned to face him. "I've never met anyone quite like her. The more sure she is about something, the more likely it is she's wrong. Where did she dream up all these theories about old people?"

"With your experience, maybe you should write a book."

The telephone rang and he held up his hand, wanting to be on the extension when she answered. They synchronized it pretty well. She was saying hello just as he got the instrument to his ear. Silence, but not complete silence. He was aware of someone breathing. Is this what obscene phone calls sound like? Then the line went dead. He went back to the kitchen where Susan still stood with the phone in her hand, a bewildered expression on her face.

"Hang it up."

"Was it him?"

"We'll see."

He didn't like it. He went upstairs and used the shortwave to contact Wayne. Only Wayne didn't reply. He could see the car's fender as before, but he couldn't raise him on the radio. He could use the phone to call downtown and have them try to reach him by radio, but he didn't want the phone tied up. There would be another call, he was sure of it.

"Yo." It was Wayne.

"Where you been?"

"Stretching my legs."

"Your day is just beginning."

"What's up?"

"The money's here. There's been a call. Nothing said, just checking. They may be on their way."

"Casey and Lorch?"

"You'll be the first to know."

"I don't think they've got the imagination."

"If only they'd read *Mad*."

He went downstairs to the kitchen, where Susan sat patiently at the table. She was taking this very well. She had been through a lot in these past days, but there were no signs that she was falling apart. He felt guilty because he looked forward to seeing her, as if doing his job was a way of being unfaithful to Ginny. He had the damnedest conversations with Susan.

"Tell me about being married," she said when he had dealt and they were studying their hands.

He looked at her. "You tell me. You've been married."

"It's been so long I hardly remember. Fred was Fred, an old man, cranky, not at all like living with a man. I try to think of what it was like with Harry, someone I could really talk to, someone close . . ."

It gave Morley a glimpse into the loneliness of the single, the widowed, the divorced. It had to be harder when you'd known the difference, no matter that Susan said she couldn't remember.

"Someone to fight with."

She gave a little laugh. "I even miss that. Of course, I had fights with Fred."

"It's not the same."

"What's she like?"

Ginny? "If Harry was alive and I asked about him, what would you say?"

"We wouldn't be talking if Harry was alive."

"You mean Fred."

"I'm sorry I asked."

They went back to cards. If Ginny overheard this he'd never hear the end of it. Or he would. She had gained too many points over the Widow Brady, he was at a permanent disadvantage. Maybe if she would misbehave, they'd be even again. Phyllis. Hanging around with Phyllis was almost as bad. Phyllis was trouble.

"Being married is more like living with Fred than you remember."

What a ding-dong conversation to be having while they were waiting here for a couple of crooks to call about the ten thousands dollars her bank had sent over. He pushed back from the table. The movement seemed to cause the doorbell to ring. Amy Rordam.

"I'll check on Wayne," Morley said, and retreated upstairs.

4

WILL TONSOR sat on his patio pondering a dilemma. He was a man in need of a woman; that was one of the givens of his life, a fact he had faced some years before. He had sought to remedy this lack and failed, but now, belatedly, two paths stretched before him, each presumably leading to the desired goal.

On the one hand was the elusive Amy Rordam. Relying on his own estimate of the matter, Will would have concluded long since that he was wasting his time and hers, but those who must know better than he insisted that stout heart would eventually win fair lady. And, of course, Amy's spurning of every approach stimulated rather than cooled his ardor, thanks to the assurances of Susan Nebens and Matt Hilliard. One such authority alone he might have doubted, but the judgments of a roué like the club pro and of a sensible widow like Susan Nebens overrode his own limited and, in any case, untrustworthy experience.

On the other hand there was Brenda Bowles, the plump librarian with the pushy, pneumatic breasts who was undeniably drawn to Will Tonsor.

"I don't read much," he had confessed, falling into conversation with her when there was no sign of Amy in the library.

"Some read, others do." She shifted her weight and there was a mysterious rustle of silk, a whiff of perfume. "For some people books are a substitute for life."

"Do you read much?"

She kept her head down when she lifted her eyes. Will got his off her breasts just before their gazes met.

"What else is there for people our age to do in Belting?"

The suggestion that he was as young as Brenda, whose mint-flavored breath seemed to come in pants, emboldened him.

"I'll look into it."

"I'm in the book." She put her hand on his. "The phone book."

Will felt like leaning across the counter and pressing his lips to hers. He wanted to feel her, hold her, run his hands through her hair. He had the distinct feeling that she would not object to such explorations.

No wonder he sat on his patio wondering what to do. From Brenda he was getting a clear come-on, from Amy he was getting the cold shoulder. The solution seemed obvious, but he dreaded turning to Brenda only to learn that Hilliard and Susan had indeed been right and Amy Rordam might have been his. Brenda represented fun but Amy had spunk. Will relished the thought of being ordered about by that little lady, being looked after. Brenda would cling and how much of that was he up to at his age?

Things were complicated now because Amy felt obliged to spend much of her time with Susan. Poor Susan, Will

Tonsor said aloud, trying out the thought he assumed Amy and others had. He himself found it difficult to feel sorry for her because she was rid of that crotchety old bastard Fred Nebens. If it had fallen to Will Tonsor to look after a daughter-in-law, he would not have kept her tied down in Belting, Wisconsin, by God. They would have traveled, seen the world, expanded their horizons. But Fred had clung to a wheelchair, whining and making a burden of himself. Still, it was kind of Amy to be concerned.

Despite what he felt about Fred, he too could be concerned. The thought was calculating. Amy's defenses could be broken through by Will Tonsor's sympathy for her young friend. And, after all, Susan was his ally in this pursuit. She would no doubt put in a good word for him at crucial moments. Here was a course of action that could be taken despite his dilemma. He would become Susan Nebens's protector and in this role he could only rejoice that Amy was a frequent presence in Susan's house.

PART EIGHT

1

LORCH WAITED until Casey was out of sight. In the back seat, the woman tried to get the door open, but he had all the doors locked and controlled them from up front. The windows too. He counted to three out loud after Casey was no longer visible, then tromped on the gas. He was free of that little sonofabitch at last.

The freedom he'd dreamed of off and on since going in with Casey was a bit confusing at first now that he had it, maybe because the woman wouldn't stop yelling.

"Shut up," he advised her. He turned on the radio, rock at full blast, to drown her out.

He could just drive, the way he had with Casey, switching cars, going south, getting away from trouble. But he would leave a trail. He had already left a trail. How many stolen cars had he stashed around this burg already? The first thing, the trail had to stop.

"Please turn down the radio."

She had to shout to make herself heard, but she didn't sound hysterical. Lorch had a tin ear, and he hated rock after listening to it for years whether he wanted to or not. He turned off the radio.

He had to get rid of the car and then get out of here by bus or train. Go home. Home. Where the hell was home? Anywhere away from Casey would do. The main thing was the trail had to end; no more cars and he'd be clean. The girl was the problem now. What he'd done could be called kidnapping, worse trouble than trying to shake down a widow for the money they were supposed to have gotten driving a load of grass to Chicago.

When he looked in the rearview mirror he found the woman was staring at him. Their eyes met in the mirror. She had calmed down. Lorch found it too easy to imagine her in court identifying him as the man who had forced her into a car and driven away with her. Without his previous record that might have been nothing. He could just let her out now and drive off and that would be it. But it wouldn't be forgotten, not with Lorch at the wheel. Besides Casey would sing first chance he got and if there was one thing sure it was that Casey would be busted sooner or later, most likely sooner. Lorch realized he was doomed. He'd been doomed since he went partners with Casey. Sometimes he felt he had been doomed since he dropped out of De La Salle.

"Where are you taking me?"

He ignored her. He had no answer at the moment anyway. Casey's recommendation would have been obvious so it was a good thing Casey had the gun with him. Guns weren't his style anyway. You don't need a gun to shut someone up.

He was imagining Casey talking. He should never have listened to that little monkey, strutting around, adjusting his belt, wobbly in his goddam cowboy boots. First there was the easy money they were going to make because Casey had heard Rains talking in Stillwater. And all they found was a field of corn. Then there'd been the widow and her ten thousand. And they ended up with sandwiches.

"Tell me something," Lorch said, not looking at the broad.

"You're not going back for him, are you?"

Casey? Hell no. "When you brought the sack of food, you came from the house, right?"

"Why do you ask?"

"I wanna know was there ever any money talked about."

"The ten thousand dollars?"

He had his eye on her in the mirror and he couldn't tell if she was lying. Casey would have monkeyed with his belt, giving a clue, but how did this broad signal when she lied?

"It's still there. The bank sent it over, the way you wanted it. The mailman brought it. That's why I thought you were policemen watching the house."

Lorch's mind was running. He gave Casey a hard time, but the fact was he preferred having someone else figuring out what was to be done. On his own, he had no confidence. But he thought of that ten thousand in the widow's house, just waiting to be picked up. How long had it been since the broad arrived with the sandwiches? Fifteen, twenty minutes. He and Casey might still be there, staked out, waiting to go for the money.

"You could still get it," she said.

He tossed his shoulders in a silent laugh, but she leaned forward, putting her elbows on the back of the front seat.

"Take me back there and I'll bring it out. The way I did the sandwiches."

"You'd do that for me?"

"What do you plan to do with me otherwise?"

He glanced at her. Smart dame. A smart dame who counted on him being dumb. Sure, she would just waltz in and toss him the money and wish him on his way.

"There's a stakeout."

"Wayne. I know him. I can take care of him."

"Tell me about it."

He should have been as skeptical listening to Casey. This broad who wanted him to know her name was Amanda would tell Wayne it was okay and they would go on to the house and the money was just waiting. Like Casey she was vague on details. Lorch didn't believe a word she said.

But he headed the car back toward the house of Susan Nebens.

2

THE STREET was lined with cars ready for the taking, but Casey would have to find one with the door unlocked and the keys in it. Lorch, the sonofabitch, had the knack, no two ways about that. Just picked a car and took it, no sweat.

He stood there, still half hoping Lorch would pull up to the curb and they'd drive off. No need to mention his notion that Lorch had ditched him. Just because the car wasn't right here where he'd gotten out didn't mean Lorch was gone for good. He could have all kinds of reasons for going around the block. And how was he to know Casey could do it all that quick, be back here so soon? Maybe he wanted to switch cars. Lorch was always big on that, never keep the same car for long.

Lorch didn't show. Casey hadn't really thought he would. From the moment he got back he knew Lorch was gone. With the broad. Thinking about that, Casey began to grin, letting the smile form slowly on his narrow face. Suddenly he felt good. Lorch was stuck with her and that was a real rap. By contrast, Casey was as good as clean. After all, what had he done? It was Lorch who kept taking other people's cars. What the hell was he supposed to do, turn him in? The more he thought of it, the more it looked as if Lorch had done him one helluva big favor by calling it quits.

Getting mad about the cornfield and the sack of sandwiches left Lorch with the girl. If Lorch had any sense, which he didn't, he'd shut her up for good. Casey patted his side. At least he still had the gun. And his clothes. And the hula girl lamp. He was still grinning when a cab slid past. The driver grinned back and Casey stopped the cab.

The driver turned out to be a broad who looked and talked like a man, and Casey didn't like that at all.

"Where to, cowboy?"

Her license said she was Mitzi Glick, her hair was greasier than Lorch's and she had a cigarette in the corner of her mouth.

"Just roll, will you, Mitzi. I'm trying to think of the address."

"Looks like you're moving."

"Yeah."

"Old lady throw you out?"

"I left. Nobody throws me out."

"What kind of lamp is that?"

"You like it?" He held it up. "You should see her plugged in."

"Yeah."

He wouldn't have bet on it when he first laid eyes on her, but he got along with Mitzi. She figured he'd broken up with his old lady and that got her going on divorce, about which she considered herself an expert. She'd been married three times and wasn't likely to do it again. Trouble with divorce, nobody wins.

"I mean nobody. You probably think she's got the edge on you, right? Alimony? Or she got the house? The car? Leaving you to take cabs. Well, let me tell you the other side of the equator."

The other side was that Mitzi hadn't got tiddly squat from any of hers. The first time, she got support and the house, but he just bugged out and she was left holding a mortgage. Any equity went to the realtors when she got rid of the dump; in fact she lost money. Her second had nothing in the first place and for a year afterward kept coming around putting the bite on her.

"My third's in prison."

"Yeah?"

"For good. Well, for life. It all came as news to me. He said he'd been in the Merchant Marine. Turned out he'd spent most of his life behind bars. Habitual. He'll never get out."

"So you divorced him?"

"Oh, I visit him."

Casey bet the guy would too see the outside again, but it was a familiar story. Women didn't want to stay married to a con. Women didn't like to come visit a man caged up like an animal. And neither wanted any kids to see a guy in that condition. The con always thought he'd been shafted and Casey understood that. But he understood the woman too.

He got his bearings and Mitzi went where he told her—why not, with the goddam meter running?—and he didn't get it right at first. The trouble with just riding is you don't really watch where you're going; you let the driver worry about it. But a big street that looked familiar was, and soon they were going in what Casey was sure was the right direction.

"You live out here?"

"It's a nice neighborhood."

Mitzi didn't have to act that surprised. The idea was he was a guy who'd fought with his wife and was on his way home to make one more stab at making up. Casey got so caught up in this bullshit he half believed it himself. Susan Nebens became the wife who'd thrown him out. Well, she'd thrown out the old guy, thrown him out with the trash. And that was why she was going to pay Casey money.

The sandwiches had been a mistake. That much the broad made clear. It hadn't been a trick. He would have talked Lorch into going back again, and this time they would get the ten thousand. Only it was going to be Casey alone.

They got to the neighborhood, and a block away from the house he had Mitzi go around a corner and pull over.

"This it?"

"Mitzi, I'll level with you. What I want is to pick up some tools I don't want her to have. I mean, I need them, understand? I just want to slip in the house, pick up those tools and I'll be back like a shot."

Mitzi turned and gave him the fish eye. "You figure on grabbing the kids, is that it?"

"No! No kids. She can have the kids. The kids are hers, not ours. You wait here and I'll be back. Look, I'll leave my stuff here. It won't take but five minutes. Ten at most."

He got out and stood by the driver's door, looking down at Mitzi. She reminded him of one of the guards at Stillwater. What the hell could she do but wait? She wasn't getting paid otherwise.

"Keep the meter running."

"Don't worry."

"And watch that lamp."

3

WHEN THE driver drove off after the other man had cut through a parking lot and out of sight, Amanda was at first more terrified than before. From the beginning, she had the sickening certainty these men intended to rape and then kill her. She meant nothing to them. They were animals, she was sure of it. But within a block, alone with Lorch, she sensed this was a situation she could control. Her initial reaction had been understandable, God knows, anyone would have been terrified, man or woman. After all, they had kidnapped her.

And trying to get out had made sense, to escape, but the door was locked and every time she lowered the window, he raised it. The music was the worst part, but the very cacophony had enabled her to think. From the moment he turned off the radio, Amanda felt in control. What was the situation?

These were the men who had somehow persuaded Susan to take ten thousand dollars from the bank and turn it over to them.

They had been waiting in their parked car because they wanted to see how Susan got the money. They were not aware that the mailman had brought the money.

Lorch had perked up when she told him the money was at the house. And suddenly this initially terrifying event was transformed into the opportunity of her professional lifetime. She would lead Lorch back to the house where he would be taken into custody. And she could inform Paul Morley where the accomplice had been dropped off.

Of course Lorch knew the police were watching the place, she'd told him that, but now Wayne too seemed a character in her scenario. She would persuade Wayne to let her go by . . . No, she would just stop and chitchat, giving Lorch the impression that arrangements were being made. No need to tell Wayne what she was doing. Paul Morley would be her collaborator in this deed. She would let him decide precisely how it was to be done. Amanda imagined herself returning from the house, carrying the money as she had carried the sandwiches, her progress anxiously followed, as she set Lorch up. Dangerous? Of course. But what a coup it would be, taking part in the capture of one of Fred Nebens's killers. As far as she could see, Lorch was unarmed.

They got to the house sooner than Amanda would have expected.

"You know, we could go right in the driveway," Amanda suggested.

He ignored her, pulling over to the curb just behind Wayne. Obviously he didn't want any changes now.

"Unlock the door."

He turned and looked at her, and she felt again the sickening fear she had known when she was first shoved into this car. But then the latch snapped and she pressed down the handle and pushed the door open.

"I'll say something to Wayne and go on to the house."

He nodded.

Amanda closed the door carefully and walked up to the old Pontiac in which Wayne was slumped behind the wheel reading. Hadn't he noticed the car pull in behind?

"Wayne," she whispered.

He lifted his great blue eyes to her, but abruptly his expression changed. Amanda's wrist was grasped at the same time that Lorch's fist went into Wayne's face. There was a struggle between the two men that was soon over. Lorch now held the gun he had taken from Wayne. His face was expressionless. He led the stunned Amanda around the car to the passenger seat. He got in back.

"We are now going into the driveway, Wayne. Got it?"

Wayne nodded.

"So start the goddam engine."

He did.

"Slowly now. Into the driveway, then stop but keep the motor running. And you, Amanda, you're gonna go in and bring out the money, got it? You're going to do that because you don't want anything to happen to Wayne. Am I right?"

Amanda nodded. All her thoughts of being the heroine in what was about to happen had fled. Wayne pulled into the driveway and came to a stop. He turned and looked at her before she got out.

"I'll be back," she promised.

4

WILL TONSOR paused and looked out over the neat rectangle of lawn bordered by chain-link fence that it was his pleasure to survey from his patio. It is a fundamental male role to protect the female of the species, and Will was relishing his resolution to watch over Susan and, into the bargain, the elusive Amy Rordam. That Amy might be impressed by his concern was not his primary motive, but thinking of Amy's likely reaction certainly did not deter him.

Will stepped into his kitchen, took a diet cola from the refrigerator, and poured half of it into a glass. It was a concoction that commended itself only because of its low caloric content. The sweetener in it dried his mouth, and he had to pee minutes after drinking the stuff. But it was also conducive to thought. He went onto the patio, sat on the edge of a chair and thought.

He found that he was excited by the image of himself as

the protector of Amy. It seemed to him now that he had always been gallant, a knight errant ready to take on the forces of evil. Dramatic? Perhaps. But life is dramatic, or ought to be. It was what he wished to convince Amy of. The great danger of their age was to look backward, remember, cry over spilt milk. But Will Tonsor was dedicated to the present moment, the time in which he now lived. The future might be as uncertain as the state lottery, but no one could take away the present. And oh how he would like to share his present with Amy Rordam.

Yes, indeed. He would keep an eye on her. His all-but-lashless eyes narrowed. How could he not be influenced by the television fare he enjoyed? That a fragile old man could sit by the hour, identifying himself with heroes who engaged in brawls, high-speed car chases and generally intemperate living might seem odd, but Will Tonsor transposed all this superactivity into a key his imagination could play.

And so it was that, an hour later, he sat in his parked car up the street from Susan's house, slumped behind the wheel, a felt hat retrieved from mothballs pulled low over his eyes.

When he was a kid, Will had climbed a tree in his parents' front yard and from his perch on a high branch watched the world below. Why are things looked at from secrecy more mysterious? All in the eye of the beholder perhaps. Looked at from under the brim of his hat through narrowed eyes, the street took on an air of strangeness, as if something extraordinary might happen at any moment. But have no fear, Will Tonsor would be on guard duty.

Some time later he came awake with a start, but in a moment he was oriented. Susan Nebens's house, of course. He stirred uneasily. Asleep at his post. A capital offense in wartime, wasn't it? He rubbed his eyes and looked at the house. Half-pulled shades gave its windows the look of sleepy eyes. He yawned. It was an hour of day when he liked his nap. He earned it with his morning run. He called himself to order with thoughts of Amy. Odd that her father and brother had been such losers.

When Will asked Matt Hilliard if he remembered a Rordam on the grounds crew of the club the golf pro threw his putter into the air. He caught it expertly, but maintained his expression of exaggerated alarm.

"I had hoped never to hear that name again."

"He was pretty bad?"

"Is burning out six greens the day before the city tournament bad enough for you?"

"He did that?"

"Not that he remembered it. He was drunk all the time. That's why he wasn't badly injured when he drove the big fairway mower through the caddy shack. We had caddies then. We also still had members who were scared of unions. Rordam was union. Teamsters. He organized the local himself. Three members. But he could have called out the waitresses, the cook, stopped deliveries to the club. A drunk with power. That's my definition of a fascist."

"Why did he leave?"

A smile played on Hilliard's lips, a mean smile, a satisfied smile. "Any man, drunk or sober I don't care, *any* man can be brought down by sex."

Will Tonsor sought more comfort in the chair he sat in. Hilliard had the look of a bard about to intone an epic. The long and the short of it was that Rordam had been undone when Hilliard and the caddymaster stashed him stoned in the women's dressing room, in a shower, naked. He woke up in a rampant condition and walked into a sea of startled and soon screaming women. It was a Monday. Ladies Day at the club. Two women were eager to testify that Rordam had assaulted them, but the shamefaced and already flaccid Rordam who fled into the men's locker room where Hilliard and Zemac, the caddymaster, awaited him was no threat in that department to anyone. Rordam had been cashiered at a meeting of the full membership and there hadn't been a peep from any union.

"I am in love with his sister."

Hilliard closed, then opened his eyes. "Is this the little lady we've been discussing of late?"

"Amy Rordam."

"What about that librarian?"

But Will Tonsor was not to be deflected now. He had dismissed Hilliard's stories. The sins of the brother must not be visited upon the sister. And the father had bequeathed Amy her sturdy bungalow.

A glance at his watch told Will that, far from nodding off, he had taken a nap of a half hour's duration. Ye gods. He stared at the house. Could Amy have left while he was dozing? Once he had admitted the question, he could not dismiss it, not least because there was no way to answer it by simply staring at the house. His large hand dropped to the cellular phone mounted between the bucket seats. But before he could activate Susan's number, which he had had the foresight to program into the instrument, a battered car came swiftly toward him, seemed determined to run into him head on but swerved into the driveway and came to a stop by the kitchen door.

5

THEIR NAMES were Lorch and Casey, according to Paul
Morley, and of course he thought they were responsible for
Fred's death.

"What I don't understand is the way they killed him. Or
why. At least until after they got some money out of you,"
said Morley, eyeing his cards.

Susan regarded the ten thousand dollars as punishment for
what she had done. No one would believe her now if she
told the truth, but eventually she would have to. She could
not let those men be blamed for something they had not
done, even if they were convicts.

"What were their crimes?"

Theft, armed robbery. They had never harmed anyone before;
they never stole enough money to make it worth the bother.

"Because they're dumb," Paul Morley said complacently.
"Prisons are full of dumb bunnies who think they're smart."

"They never harmed anyone?"

"Not until now."

"I don't think they killed Fred."

"Well, he's dead."

Run over by Susan's own car. The police investigation had established that. Paul expected her to be surprised and she obliged. Oh what a tangled web she was weaving. But not as tangled as the account Paul Morley gave.

"Can they tell how long it had been since Fred died?"

"Not anymore. It's your deal."

Susan had gone alone when Fred was cremated. The urn of his ashes was in the garage, awaiting disposal.

"Sprinkle my ashes over your roses," Fred had said more than once, his tone melancholy, rolling his eyes to her, inviting sympathy at the thought that all too soon he would be dead.

"I thought you didn't like this garden."

"It's just a suggestion."

"You own a burial plot." Next to the wife who had died when Harry was sixteen.

"With all the traffic going by that place?"

Another conversation that didn't make much sense. Given the way things had turned out, Susan felt bound by Fred's offhand remark. So she had him cremated and eventually would scatter his ashes over her roses. The roses continued to bloom, but soon their season would be over. In the meantime, she was almost as sheepish about having his ashes in the garage as she had been when his body had lain on the stack of newspapers.

If Fred still survived somewhere, he would be seething about the Unitarian minister who said a few words before the cremation, not really a ceremony.

"What was that you read?" Susan asked her.

"Wallace Stevens."

"I didn't understand it."

The Reverend Roberta Stich looked expressionlessly at Susan. "He sold insurance."

Well, he would have starved as a poet, in Susan's estimation. There might be lots of ways of looking at a blackbird, but none of them seemed appropriate to the occasion. It served her right for ignoring Fred's very vocal agnosticism.

"If there is a God he wouldn't have anything to do with those bozos." Fred was watching the religious channel, a favorite of his.

"Judge not," Susan said.

"They're a judgment on themselves."

Like most nonchurchgoers, Fred was obsessed with organized religion. He listened through a televised sermon of Roberta Stich without complaint.

"Not much to disagree with there. Unitarians believe there is at most one god. I used to cut the hair of the Episcopal bishop. He told me that one."

"At your age you might think of putting your house in order."

"Ha. If God can be fooled that easily . . ."

He didn't finish the thought. There were limits to what Fred was likely to say, on the supposition that, if God existed, he was listening in and He was bigger than Fred. It was on that slim premise that Susan had based her decision to contact Reverend Roberta Stich.

"He was a fan of yours."

"Did I know him?"

"He was housebound."

A term he'd hated. If only he had stayed in the house when she was getting the car out to take him to the doctor. Oh, what she wouldn't give to be able to live over again those crucial moments when, instead of telephoning for an ambulance, she had picked up Fred's body and carried it into the garage. It had been an unplanned deed, done almost without thinking, yet from it had flowed a series of events, culminating in the assumption that the two ex-convicts who were trying to extort money from her had killed Fred. What would Paul Morley say when those two explained they were asking Susan to pay for their silence? When they claimed Fred's body had been in the car they stole, long since dead, could this be proved now that the body was cremated? It was Susan's hope that they would get the money and disappear. Ten thousand dollars was an awful price to pay for the return of her peace of mind, but more and more it seemed worth it.

When Amy arrived, Susan and Paul Morley stopped playing cards, largely because she urged them to continue. Go ahead, have fun, don't mind me. She was still peeved that she hadn't been invited to Fred's final services.

"There wasn't anything you could call a service, Amy."

"No readings?"

Clearly Amy would not be impressed to hear about Wallace Stevens and the blackbird. Nor by a description of the efficiency with which things were done at the crematorium. Dignified and impersonal. That too was what Fred had said he'd wanted.

"I don't want people who hardly knew me pretending to be sad."

Bravura, Susan decided. Who were these "people" supposed to be, apart from herself, Amy and Will Tonsor?

"No parade either?"

He pretended he hadn't heard her, a ploy he used when he had no ready retort. Well, if nothing else she had fulfilled his wishes.

"Will Tonsor is parked up the street," Amy said with disgust.

"What on earth for?"

"The Lord only knows. I think he has some crazy notion that he is looking after you."

"You must tell Paul Morley."

"I'll do no such thing. If Will Tonsor insists on making an ass out of himself, it is no concern of mine."

"Then I'll tell him."

Paul Morley had been angry enough when Amy showed up. If Lorch and Casey couldn't wait and were dumb enough to come to the house for the money, he didn't want a lot of people around who could get hurt. Not that he thought they'd actually get to the house. As soon as they showed up in the neighborhood, they'd be taken into custody.

Amy and Susan were at the kitchen table and Paul upstairs when there was the sound of a car in the driveway and a moment later Amanda burst in.

6

AFTER USING the upstairs bathroom Paul Morley went into the front bedroom to check out Wayne. This must have been Fred's bedroom. A sour old man's smell lingered in the spick-and-span room. Now Susan would be all alone in the house.

When he looked into the street, he saw the Pontiac approach with accelerating speed and then swing into the driveway. What the hell.

He went into the hall and down the stairs to the landing where he could see the top of the Pontiac from the windows overlooking the driveway. Someone in the back seat. A man. The kitchen door opened and Amanda spoke.

"Where's the money?" Her voice was high and excited.

Morley looked again at the Pontiac below. Something was wrong. He went up to the second floor again and into the back bedroom. This was definitely Susan's room. A photograph of Harry Nebens regarded him reproachfully from the dresser. The window looked out over the roof of the back porch and beyond at the garden. Paul Morley eased it up, slowly, listening to the lead weight in the old casement move. The screen was affixed to the frame from outside. He got out his pocketknife, plunged it through the rusty screen, brought it downward to make an incision large enough for his hand. Gripping the mesh, he pulled it aside, making the opening he was going to have to get through.

Suddenly a figure materialized in the back yard, coming through the hedge, with a gun in his hand. Morley stepped back from the window. What the hell was going on?

He turned and ran down the stairs and burst into the kitchen where Amanda, Susan and Amy were fighting over the sack containing ten thousand dollars.

"Where's Wayne?"

Amanda turned to him, wild-eyed. "In the car. Lorch took away his gun. I've got to give him this."

But even as she spoke, Susan took possession of the sack. "I will turn over the money."

Amy cried, "Susan, you can't go out there."

Susan pulled open the door, but before she could leave Wayne was shoved through it. He stumbled across the kitchen and fell to the floor, taking Amanda with him. The man who followed Wayne was flourishing a gun. Lorch. Not the one who'd come through the back hedge. Morley lifted his weapon, but Susan and Amy were in his line of fire. Hesitation was costly. A roar and then a bullet slammed into Morley's arm. His gun fell to the floor.

Lorch grabbed the sack of money, getting Susan's hand with it. He pulled her out the door and Amy followed, hanging onto Susan.

"Do something!" Amanda screamed.

Wayne scrambled to this feet, snatched up Morley's gun as he rose and started for the door. From outside came the sound of more gunfire.

"Someone's in the back yard," Wayne said. "I think it's Casey."

But this did not mean reinforcements for Lorch. Casey came between the porch and the garage, grinning like a skull, holding his gun with both hands. He was trying to get off another shot, but Lorch had scooted around the car and out of sight. Susan and Amy took refuge in the back seat of the Pontiac. Morley pulled Wayne back inside lest Casey take him as a target of opportunity.

Lorch stood up and got off a lucky shot. There was a howl of pain. A second shot silenced Casey, and Lorch turned his weapon on the house and Morley and Wayne got out of the doorway. With a rattling roar the Pontiac backed rapidly down the drive, straightened out and barreled up the street.

7

WILL TONSOR watched with open mouth as the car roared down the driveway and careened across the lawn and into the street. A shifting of gears, and then it shot by with Susan and Amy in the back seat with one of the plainclothes policemen driving. What in the hell was going on?

Will's hand had twisted the ignition key of its own accord and the sound of the motor surprised him. He grabbed the hat from the seat beside him and clamped it on his head as if it were the uniform of the day and he was useless without it. He started forward, turned into the Nebens' driveway, backed into the street and drove off in the direction Susan had gone, but there was no sign now of the battered Pontiac. At the corner, he stopped. Which way should he turn? He decided to go left, but once he entered the intersection he changed his mind and spun the wheel to the right. If they were heading for police headquarters, they would have gone right.

But there was no sign of the Pontiac. Will Tonsor was torn between driving fast, to catch up, and driving slowly, lest he had made a mistake and was increasing the distance between himself and Susan. Susan and Amy. Something about the sight of Amy in the back seat bothered him. Undercover cops looked like that, of course, as anyone who watched television knew. But why had Amy looked so terrified? She was being taken away from the shooting. The more Will thought of it, the less he liked it. He pulled over to the curb and put through a call to the police.

"Did you send a man to the Nebens home a short while ago."

"Who is this?"

A kid on the sidewalk was staring at Will, fascinated by the telephone. "A friend."

"A friend of who?"

"Who am I talking to?"

"The police."

"Do you have a name?"

"You go first."

Will felt that he was being made fun of and that the boy on the sidewalk knew it. "This is not a game! I have to know if the man I saw at the Nebens home was a policeman."

"When was this?"

"Five minutes ago!"

"Where you calling from?"

"My automobile."

A pause. "Where is your automobile?"

"On East Ontario."

"How can you see the Nebens house from there?"

"I just drove away from the house."

"Give me your name."

Furious, Will cut the call. The presumed policeman he had just telephoned seemed no more genuine than the one he had seen at Susan's house. A dizzying thought. Had that been a cop in the car with Amy and Susan? The boy who had been watching him edged nearer to the car, trying to see where Will had put the phone. All Will's pique was suddenly directed at the kid. He lowered the window on the passenger side.

"Get away from the car!"

The kid stared in at him slack-mouthed.

"Get out of here," Will shouted.

The boy raised his hand in slow motion and gave Will an insolent single-fingered salute.

8

IN THE back seat, Amy could not stop squealing and crying.

"Cut it out," Lorch shouted at her. "Nobody's done nothing to you. What're you crying about?"

He feinted a blow with the gun and Amy ducked out of harm's way.

"Where are we going?" Susan asked. His expression told her he hadn't the faintest idea. "Why don't you quit while you're ahead. I know you didn't kill Fred."

His wild eyes found hers. "Did you?"

She nodded.

His relief lasted only seconds. "They saw me do Casey."

"That was self-defense."

"You a lawyer?"

But his mind wasn't on the conversation. He was a desperate man, gone beyond the point when he could turn back. Perhaps he had passed that point many years ago. Driving with the gun in his hand was clumsy. He threw it on the seat beside him. Susan leaned forward.

"You're in enough trouble now."

"Then I've got nothing to lose, have I?"

"All right. But you have that money." Bills of various denominations spilled from the sack he'd tossed into the car before shooting Casey. "You have to let Amy go."

"I don't have to do anything."

"I'll tell them you killed my father-in-law."

His eyes smoldered when she met them in the mirror. "You saw what happened to Casey when he got funny with me. Just keep it up."

"Go to the bank and I'll draw out more money."

If only he would stop, Amy could slip out and run away and be safe and off her conscience. Susan felt that she herself deserved whatever happened, because of what she had done to Fred, because of what she had let others believe had happened.

"Don't be funny."

"I am not being funny. We can stop at the drive-in window and . . ."

"Forget the goddam bank."

But the idea had caught hold of his imagination. That sack of money looked pathetic lying there. How could he think that more would provide him with a shield, power, a magic carpet on which to ride right out of the mess he was in?

"Tell me how you'd do it."

He had slowed down now. They were miles from any branch of her bank. But, for the first time, Susan believed she could handle Lorch. Having given him directions, she put her arms over the front seat and told him in great detail how things would go when they got to the bank. He had never been to a drive-in window before.

"I'll have to sit up front, so they can see me."

He was much calmer now. They seemed to have sped out of trouble. There were no wailing sirens, no signs of any police vehicles. He pulled over and waited for her to move into the front seat. When she got in, the ten thousand dollars and his pistol still lay on the seat where they had been.

"How much money you got?"

"More than you need. You should get as far away from here as you can."

"You worried about me?" A cruel crooked smile twisted his lips.

Amy's whimpering annoyed Susan almost as much as it did Lorch, or it did until she reminded herself she was responsible for Amy's being here and in danger of her life. The poor thing. Of course she was terrified. Susan was terrified herself. She knew what this animal had done to his partner. And he had shot at Paul Morley and then at Wayne. For all she knew they were wounded and bleeding. Or dead.

Her breath caught at the thought, and Lorch glanced at her and slowed the car more. Had he thought their speed worried her? A considerate killer. But she felt a match for him now. She moved her purse beyond the gun, then groped for and found it. She slid it behind her back. Now she was armed, for what that was worth. She had never shot a weapon more powerful than a .22 in her life, but she had often gone with Harry to the pistol range, where she learned to hit the target more often than she missed it. It had surprised her how the pistol lifted as she fired, sending the bullet high above the concentric circles of the paper target twenty-five yards away. Correcting for that tendency had been her main concern as she concentrated on the target. Susan doubted that she could point a weapon at another human being.

"After the bank, I'll go with you."

"You got no choice."

"Please let Amy go." They were on Cleveland Road, approaching the bank. "You only need one hostage, you don't need her."

"Hostage? You jumped into the car of your own free will."

"That's true. I'll tell them that."

"Tell who?"

"Everyone. After you're gone."

Amy didn't help by choosing that moment to burst more loudly into tears. Susan turned sideways on the seat toward Lorch. He hunched over the wheel now, looking thoughtfully ahead.

"How far."

"It's in the mall."

"How far's that?"

"Just ahead." She had never been good at distances. A mile, two? But when they came to the mall, he did not turn in.

"This is it!"

But he just shook his head. Susan could have cried she was so disappointed. She had been so sure he would follow her directions. But his mind was made up. He was not going to drive into a bank with two frightened women in the car. Too much could happen in circumstances unfamiliar to him. She understood him even as she groaned in disappointment. He pressed on the gas pedal. Somewhere ahead there must be some place, any place, where Amy could be set free. It would have been too good if he had driven into the bank where Amy could easily have slipped out the door. Had he imagined that Amy would sound the alarm, find a phone and tell the police where he was? The wailing Amy in the back seat did not seem to Susan to pose a threat to anyone.

From the road, the mall seemed the very symbol of normalcy, its vast parking lots filled, the long, low building studded with the logos of the different stores, the generally festive air that the idea of shopping brought with it. How wonderful it would be to wander from store to store and satisfy the acquisitive impulse, as carefree as all the other shoppers. But the sight of a yellow dumpster destroyed the impression. Susan concentrated on finding a way to get Amy out of this car, safe, even if stranded in the country.

"We're being followed." Lorch had stopped leaning over the wheel and was studying the rearview mirror. Susan's heart leapt at the prospect of rescue.

"Just because there are cars behind us doesn't mean we're being followed."

"Who d'you know drives a blue Lincoln?"

"Nobody."

"Will Tonsor," Amy said, suddenly snapping out of it. She too was now looking at the road behind them. "That's Will Tonsor's car."

"Who the hell is he?"

"He's just an old man," Susan said, and her disappointment was genuine.

"Yeah? Like the other one, your father-in-law?"

"I don't think that's Will," Susan lied. If that was Will Tonsor, and it seemed to be, he would ruin the chance of getting Amy out of the car.

"I'm going to shake him."

The car lurched forward as Lorch stomped on the gas. Susan shared his hope that they would lose Will Tonsor.

He turned off Cleveland and for fifteen minutes sped along country roads. The blue Lincoln kept right with him until Lorch got onto a dirt road and the swirl of dust kicked up by the Pontiac obscured the pursuing Will. When Lorch got back on a paved road, they drove a mile, and there was no sign of the blue Lincoln behind them.

"He's gone," Lorch decided.

"What a silly old fool," Amy said, in full possession of herself. "I told you he was hanging about spying on us." But Amy's tone was not one of disapproval.

Susan wanted to let it go, but Lorch was interested. Was the old guy a cop? For answer, Amy laughed as if she hadn't a care in the world, as if it were a day or two before when Will Tonsor's infatuation could be an object of mirth or annoyance. It would have been too great a blessing for Amy to forget the danger they were in.

Lorch cut the speed and seemed about to stop the car. The road was lined now with field corn, the stalks standing ten feet high. Fodder for livestock, there was no hurry to harvest this crop. As far ahead as Susan could see, the road was empty. It seemed such a lonely place.

"Get out." Lorch was speaking to Amy.

"I am not getting out," Amy announced.

"Amy!" Susan cried. "Of course you are."

"I am not going to leave you alone with this monster."

Lorch reached back to grab her and Susan took advantage of his distraction to slip the gun into her purse. "Out you go, old lady. No need for you to ride around with a monster."

"No!"

But his patience, thank God, ran out. He reached across Amy and opened the door. Amy leaned forward and bit his wrist. He let out a yowl of pain and then shoved Amy from the car. She tumbled out and did a sort of somersault and then sat on the berm, facing the cornfield, her hair wild on her head. She turned, stunned.

"Get up," Lorch commanded. "I want you to go hide in that field until we're gone."

"Do it, Amy," Susan pleaded. Her hand was on the door and she eased down the handle. With her other hand, she gripped her purse.

Amy gave Susan a look and then glared at Lorch as she got to her feet. There was the sound of a slamming door behind them, and Susan saw Will Tonsor approaching on foot from the blue Lincoln parked behind them on the road.

"You all right, Amy?" he called.

"Will Tonsor, you get out of here." Amy, almost risen, lost her balance and fell again. Will Tonsor, lifting his knees high, moved swiftly to her, and tried to take her hand, but she kept snatching it away. Will turned toward the Pontiac.

"What's going on?"

Lorch was moving his hand around on the seat, looking for the gun. Susan pushed open her door and stepped free of the car just as he lunged for her. She fumbled with the catch of her purse. It was as if she had never opened it before, but then it had never felt so heavy before. Finally she had the gun out and pointed it at Lorch.

"I'll call the police," Will said. "I have a phone in my car."

Lorch, a disdainful sneer on his face, got out of the car on the other side. Susan lifted the pistol and pointed it at him.

"That gun is empty," Lorch said, ignoring Susan. From the trunk he took the jack and started on the run after Will Tonsor.

"Will!" Amy called. "Will Tonsor."

The tall old man stopped and turned. His expression when he saw Lorch coming at him might have been comic in other circumstances.

"Run!" Amy cried.

And run he did, lifting his knees, tucking his arms close to his side, head held high, the quintessential jogger. Graceful, perhaps, but not fast. Amy was hollering now, urging Will to hurry. But the old man might have been running in place the way Lorch closed the distance between them.

Susan looked at the gun she held. What a useless thing it was without ammunition. She threw it down in disgust and started after Lorch. She could not allow him to attack an old man.

But Will Tonsor had reached his car and was inside and behind the wheel. Lorch came to a stop before the grill and brought the jack he was carrying down on the expanse of the Lincoln's hood. Metal crumpled. He lifted the jack again. And then the Lincoln began to move. Lorch, unable to get out of the way, hopped onto the dented hood and was carried at gathering speed toward the Pontiac. Abruptly Will Tonsor braked and Lorch was propelled from the hood and tumbled onto the ground. On hands and knees, he wheeled to face Susan. The jack was still in his hand. He rose slowly, hatred in his eyes, hatred for her, hatred for the fate that had brought him to this lonely country road, humiliated by a Will Tonsor. Susan was unable to move as Lorch loomed before her, lifting the jack to strike.

There was a terrible roar in Susan's ear and the jack fell to the ground as Lorch's hands went to the great gaping wound that had been opened in his chest. Amy held the gun, her eyes squeezed tightly closed, standing as if she were about to sit down. She opened her eyes to see Lorch slump to the ground.

"I shot him," she said in wondering tones.

From his car, Will Tonsor called the police and an ambulance for Lorch. He went to Amy then, took the pistol from her and put his arms around her. Amy moved close against him and began once more to cry, but her sobs, Susan thought, now had a calculated sound.

And then Susan too began to cry with giddy relief.

PART NINE

1

IN THE weeks that followed, Amanda was a frequent visitor. She had lost interest in writing a series on the problems faced by the elderly of the nation.

"Susan, what do I know about it? What do I know about anything?"

Amanda had gone to the hospital with Wayne when he was taken in for observation. She did a bit of observation herself and seemed to decide that beneath the beard and the comic books and his dangerous job, Wayne was a man to whom she could relate.

"You mean you like him?"

"Well, yes."

Susan had no idea what they had in common. What had she and Harry had in common? But a couple makes a common life, they don't just find it. Amanda sent a story to her paper on Belting, an idealized picture of the town that won her many friends. Inquiries at the Belting *Coronet* were encouraging, and Amanda thought she might try her hand in a less demanding journalistic setting than Chicago.

"I've come to love Belting," she said, lifting lidded eyes to Wayne.

Will Tonsor told her that the cost of living index in Belting would have put it among the most desirable communities in the nation, but the citizens had no desire to draw attention to their haven.

"Look at Oregon," Will said enigmatically.

Amy sat stern-faced beside him on the couch, crocheting what seemed to be a potholder.

"Have you ever been to Oregon?" she asked.

"I read about it."

Amy made a reproving sound. Will grinned. They seemed to have established a coded form of communication no one else could fathom. Susan acted as a witness when Will and Amy married. Paul Morley agreed to be the other witness although his arm was still in a sling.

"Just so I'm not called upon to testify."

"Ha ha."

Paul had told Susan he was putting in for retirement. "After my performance when Lorch and Casey showed up, I know I'm over the hill."

Susan said nothing. It would have been cruel to point out that Amy and Will were considerably older than Paul and the two of them had quelled Lorch.

"Will you leave Belting?"

"Winters we'll spend in Florida."

"Nice."

But the thought seemed to make him gloomy. "Susan, about the attic and that, you know. I'm sorry."

There seemed nothing to say.

"That was unprofessional. I feel I jeopardized you and the others by acting like a kid."

"You weren't all that bad."

His wife didn't come to Amy and Will's wedding. Reverend Wycliff from First Presbyterian presided in the ballroom of the country club. Will had persuaded Amy that the site vindicated her family. Matt Hilliard, the pro, closed his eyes as if in pain. The bosomy woman with him was known to Amy.

"From the library," she whispered to Susan.

"Ah."

After the ceremony, when the bride and groom embraced, Paul Morley kissed Susan, but it was an end, not a beginning. Susan was glad he did it. Something would have seemed unfinished otherwise. She didn't invite Paul to the little ceremony with Fred's ashes. Amy and Will Tonsor were witnesses enough.

The three of them went into the back yard. It was November and Susan had cut back her roses and wrapped them for winter. They might have been wearing shrouds. Will Tonsor couldn't take his eyes off the urn that Susan carried to the back of the yard. There, flanked by Amy and Will, she emptied the urn. Its cloudy contents fell toward earth, but the wind sprang up and what was left of Fred Nebens flew hither and yon in the chill November air. Susan set the urn in the rose bed, not knowing what else to do with it.

"Will the hedge grow back?" Amy asked.

Casey had done considerable damage forcing his way through the hedge, as if he was determined to meet his fate.

"Whatever happened to that lamp?" Will asked, as they headed back to the house.

On that eventful day, after Lorch had driven off with

Susan and Amy, a cab had pulled into the driveway, drawn by the sound of gunfire, its meter running. Casey's things were in the back seat. They had been confiscated by the police and stashed in Susan's garage. Will Tonsor was fascinated by the lamp in the shape of a hula dancer.

"Will Tonsor," Amy said warningly.

Later, alone, her hands plunged in the pockets of her coat, Susan sat on the back porch and looked out at her yard. The empty urn stood among the winterized roses. Where was Fred?

"Ashes to ashes, dust to dust."

It was a phrase from which he had taken a mordant pleasure, repeating it more than once when he talked of the funeral he did not want. Susan formed the words silently now.

Beside her on a table, plugged in at last, the garish lamp glowed. The dancer's hips moved rhythmically, causing her skirt to sway. Fred would have liked that lamp. When Susan turned it off it was liking saying goodbye to Fred.